The Naughty or Nice Clause

The Naughty or Nice Clause

Kate Callaghan

The Naughty or Nice Clause

This is a work of fiction. Names, characters, places, and incidents either are the product of the author's imagination or are used fictitiously. Any resemblance to actual persons, living or dead, events, or locales is entirely coincidental.

First Edition November 2022

Edited by Emma O'Connell
Formatted by Enchanted Ink Publishing
Cover Design by TRC Designs

ISBN: 978-1-7397537-3-3
ISBN: 978-1-7397537-2-6
ISBN: 978-1-7397537-4-0

WWW.CALLAGHANWRITER.COM

For those who struggle through the holiday season.

I hope this story brings you some joy!

NOTE FROM THE AUTHOR

Dearest readers! I know a light and fluffy Christmas romance, minus the white wolves, isn't what you might have been expecting from me, considering my last series was about the daughter of Lucifer. It's still me – I could never completely neglect my dark side! However, after numerous Christmases going wrong, I found I had lost my Christmas spirit and began to dread the season. This book brought back some of the joy.

There is so much pressure during this time of the year. Basically, I want to give you full permission to be miserable and Grinch-like. You don't have to be happy at Christmas, and you don't have to force yourself to socialize, just because it's December. Do and feel whatever. This book was so much fun to write because so much goes wrong for the couple during what's meant to be the best time of the year. I'm delighted to share something different with you, and I hope you enjoy Lyla and Mason's Christmas adventure.

MASON & LYLA'S PLAYLIST

Loneliest Time Of The Year | Mabel

Dress | Taylor Swift

Santa Tell Me | Ariana Grande

Christmas Without You | Ava Max

Make It To Christmas | Alessia Cara

This Christmas | Picture This

Christmas | ROZES

That Way | Tate McRae

CHAPTER ONE

Fourteen days before Christmas

Lyla didn't think her day could get worse. She had torn her tights on her bike, her curls had frizzled and doubled in size thanks to the rain, and now that she had finally reached the salvation of her office, she'd found a mandate on her desk that had caused her mood to plummet to sub-zero temperatures. Her co-CEO had reared his soulless head again.

"You're looking... refreshed?" Sam, in his fuchsia suit, winced at Lyla's appearance as he placed her daily schedule on the desk. She rose, scrunching the mandate up in her hand, and her personal assistant followed her closely. "Where are you headed in such a storm?"

"Do you even need to guess?" Lyla snapped, her heels clicking on the marble floor. For weeks, she had avoided the thorn in her side – but this mandate was a war cry, one she would not take lying down. Even if it meant marching into his office before her mandatory morning coffee.

"Not happy about the mandate? The office is fuming. After the cutbacks *and* shutting down one of the toy factories, I thought he would ease up," Sam said. Lyla could smell the coffee in his cup. She resisted the urge to snatch it from his hand and down it.

"Mr Klaus? Keep his word? In the year since he's joined us, when has he ever followed through on anything positive?" she hissed, and Sam cowered a little.

"I'll leave you to the slaughter, and in case Human Resources asks about any blood stains on the carpet, I'll be sure to be your witness," he joked uneasily.

Lyla scowled. She would like nothing more than to sink her manicured nails into Mr Klaus's suit-clad muscles, which he only had thanks to his obsession with controlling everything and everyone around him.

Sam turned on his heel as soon as her hand reached out to the door handle of the office that should have been hers, but was infested with a parasite she couldn't seem to shake. She didn't bother to knock; he would already be inside. Klaus was always the first in every morning and the last to leave. When he had first joined the company she had tried to outstay him and wake up before him, but after a full month she hadn't been successful in either. She'd hated the satisfaction on his designer-stubbled face every time he'd raise a cup of coffee in teasing welcome after another humiliating defeat.

"Ms Smurfit, to what do I owe the pleasure of your presence on this glorious Monday morning?" Mr Klaus asked, leaning back in his chair. He looked perfect, as always, in a dark tailored suit, his ash-blonde hair pulled back away from his face and secured at the base of his neck. She'd thought men with hair on the longer side were supposed to be laid back, but he was anything but.

All charm this morning, she thought. If he wasn't the devil in disguise, he'd be irresistible.

The office was meticulously organised, the walls a deep teal, the bookshelves such a dark shade of wood they were almost black. *To match his soul*. A far cry from the bright colours she would have filled it with.

"You're happy this morning. Hit any small children with your car?" she snarked, walking towards the desk, not wanting anyone who might pass in the hallway to hear their conversation. She glanced over his shoulder, wondering how he could turn his back to the magnificent view of the skating rink and the giant Christmas tree at its centre. She would have turned her desk to observe the beautiful sight, while her new partner chose to turn his back on Christmas.

"I took the train into the city; my driver had a family emergency."

The world threatened to slip out from under her feet. *Has he actually done a good deed for someone?*

"But there's always hope for tomorrow morning," he continued with a smug smile before returning to his computer. *That smile.* Though it made many in the office linger at his door, she only wished to crush it under her heel. Then again, since he was such a control freak, she figured he might enjoy such an event.

Lyla took his return to work as a dismissal, but she wasn't leaving. She tapped her heel against the tiles, and his debonair smile quickly turned to a cold glare.

"The last I checked, our contract states that we are to work *with* each other. No one above or below; we make decisions together," she reminded him coldly, holding up the mandate cancelling the annual Christmas party. The Christmas party was tonight, and yet she had known nothing about the cancellation. Even the clients had apparently been informed a week before she had. At least for that she was almost grateful – if they had been informed the day of, she was sure they wouldn't have taken it lightly.

"That's certainly a pity. I do love to be on top," he commented, returning his attention to her.

"There is also a clause about sexual harassment in our contract," she remarked, slamming the mandate down in front of him. She was secretly gleeful that he had used paper; much more effective to shove in his face. Replying to an email wouldn't have had the same impact. "The Christmas party has been a tradition since my great-grandfather founded the company. We host clients and the small businesses we support. You've already shut down a factory and cut down our staff by half. Got rid of the company cars and the drivers who'd been working here for years. We make toys, for Christ's sake; how can we not celebrate Christmas?!"

"Being top of this company, I'd never harass anyone. We agreed on those changes together. Let me remind you that I own fifty-one percent of the company, so the final decision rests with me," he pointed out calmly. "You might like to play the victim in front of the staff, acting like the big bad wolf forced your hand, but we both knew those cuts would stop your precious company haemorrhaging money."

Lyla wanted nothing more than to jump across the desk and strangle him. She might be sent to prison instead of taking her rightful place as head of the company, but at least she wouldn't have to see him every day. She hated it when he talked down to her; there were only five years between them, but he made her feel six, not twenty-six.

"I know what I signed and what I agreed to. However, do I think it was extreme? Yes. Would I have done things differently and slower? Yes!"

"Let's not focus on the past," he said, his bored expression only furthering her outrage. "We've had a good year together. Let's not ruin our working relationship over something as petty as a party."

"I never wanted or agreed to my father signing over his shares," she muttered. *And our time together has been less than good.* She looked at the man who'd ruined her nights – and not in a good way – for the last three hundred and sixty-five days and counting. Not a designer button or blonde hair out of place. Every bit in control, while she felt anything but.

"Since the company is in a financial crisis, I think you should be more grateful for my signing on to take the mess off your hands," he said, folding his arms, exposing the sleek watch on his wrist. He knew money, though he wasn't flashy. She only knew the watch was designer because she'd Googled it.

She had heard of him before he had turned up. Mason Klaus, financial investor and saviour to the 1%. Lyla had no idea why he had taken on their company. It was publicly listed, but they were far from the conglomerates he usually worked with.

"What do our financial issues have to do with a Christmas party? One night for our staff and clients to have fun, to socialise. I've invited new clients, and many are interested in the smaller businesses we've absolved."

"We have enough clients with deep pockets, and we don't have the budget to take on any more mass orders," Mr Klaus disagreed.

"No one wants mass-produced anymore. We need to lean into our customers' needs, and there's no better time than Christmas. Show some company spirit! Have you never removed that damn suit and acted like a human being in your entire life?"

He raised an eyebrow. "Removing my suit? What was it you said about sexual harassment?" Apparently that was the only part of her tirade he had paid attention to.

"Cancelling is one thing, but you gave such short notice. It's embarrassing!" she exclaimed – though he *had* avoided talking about it for weeks. He'd refused to help organise or look over the budget she'd prepared, acting as though she were a lowly intern and not his partner.

"It's expensive," Klaus countered. "Catering, champagne; the staff are already receiving generous bonuses for their hard work." He turned his screen towards her with her own budget brought up, as if she didn't already know what the final figure was.

"Everyone loves Christmas, and it only happens once a year. What's the harm in splurging a little?"

"I see plenty of harm in it." He pulled the screen back to its original position.

"And you think it's fair that instead of rewarding them for their hard work, you're making them *work* Christmas Eve? I've already ordered everything, arranged the venue..." They would lose their deposits for cancelling last-minute.

"I cancelled the venue last week; the Continental was much too expensive," he said. "And your old policy was much too excessive. Twelve days off for Christmas? Absolutely insane."

"You're serious about working Christmas? Without consulting me?" She gritted her teeth, which only seemed to amuse him. "You can't blindside me with new staff policy! There's nothing to do during the season. We outsource manufacturing, so staff work from home. They aren't completely off, but it gives them flexibility during the already stressful season, and we start those twelve days with a goodbye party."

"Lyla. I'm not blindsiding you; I'm merely changing policy. That piece of paper," he pointedly shoved it towards her, "is me informing you. As much as I appreciate your enthusiasm for Christmas morale, I own the majority of the company. Christmas should be our busiest time of year, and I think this will help turn the company around. Yes, it's a sacrifice, but you have to sacrifice if you want to be successful." He opened the ledger on his desk.

Lyla closed it. "This how you imagine success – numbers on a spreadsheet? Then I'm sorry to tell you, but this isn't the company for you. People *want* to work here. We bring joy to thousands with our toys, and so we should be joyful too."

"I know why your father decided to give me his shares," he muttered under his breath. "Optimism in place of realism can only lead to failure."

Lyla took a step back, seething with fury. She almost picked up the cactus on his desk – spiky like his soul – and hurled it at his beautifully groomed jawline. Too angry to continue the conversation, she turned on her heel and marched towards the door, closing it behind her with extra vigour. His secretary eyed her sympathetically as she stalked past, but she wasn't going to take this lying down. Not when it came to Christmas.

"I told you he wouldn't budge," Sam said, sat outside her office, as she returned with her tail between her legs. She didn't mind his idleness; staff had little to do right now, since all the orders for the year had already been filled for the Christmas rush. This was their calm before next year's orders.

"No harm in trying," she reasoned, sitting on the edge of his desk. "And I'm not done fighting. We won't break tradition for one Christmas-loathing Grinch."

"I love your enthusiasm, but how exactly are you going to pull it off? I called the Continental; I may have been eavesdropping. I swear his voice could bring anyone to their knees..."

"Focus, Sam," she warned, and he rolled his eyes.

"They've already filled the space. Our clients received the cancellation notice a week ago, and most have responded to say they understand and look forward to next year." She clenched her jaw, humiliated by being the last to know. *Was I just going to show up and be alone? Then again, the staff would have arrived and been just as confused. This is a power-play on his part. Trying to show me my place as second to his. What an insufferable arse.*

"He said the event was too expensive..." It suddenly struck her. "But he never said anything about funding it ourselves. If we aren't hosting the clients, then we can have a more intimate gathering."

Sam gawked. "You want the staff to pay? And where should this gathering take place, since everywhere worth going has been booked for weeks?"

Lyla shoved him gently as they walked to the coffee machine. "No. I would never ask them to pay! Christmas is expensive enough. I'll foot the bill, and why not here? There will only be fifty or so of us – I can have the downstairs café prepare some food for this evening," she said, adding a pinch of cinnamon and nutmeg to her coffee.

"And if the Grinch hears of it? He might take you over his knee," Sam said, looking down the hall towards the monster's lair.

"Over his knee? I'd like to see him try." Lyla laughed, taking a large gulp of coffee. The caffeine hit made her all the more excited about her scheme.

"I'm sure you would." Sam grinned as they returned to her office. Her phone was ringing. "There's only a slight difference between hate and passion," he told her, before answering the phone and asking the client to hold.

"Keep any thoughts of passion to yourself. Spread the word about the party, but keep it quiet. Looks like we have to steal Christmas back," she told him, ignoring the worry in his eyes.

CHAPTER TWO

Once the day's work was done, Lyla was surprised to find that Mr Klaus had already left. *Maybe he wanted to catch the train, if his driver is out? He cuts the company cars, yet insists on having his own. Hypocrite.* Any change in his rigid schedule made her more nervous than she cared to admit. She had ordered the party food during her lunch break, and the champagne saved from the previous event had been brought up from storage.

The staff all filed up to the top floor, and they cheered when she arrived, eager to partake in the rebellion against Mr Klaus. Lyla took a bow.

"I know tonight is a rather last-minute occasion, but there was no way I wasn't marking the end of the year without celebrating all your hard work. I also decree that this is your final day of work. Go home to your families and celebrate the season."

"What about Mr Klaus? What will he say if we don't show up tomorrow?" Gemma, their social media manager, asked. The question chilled the atmosphere.

"Since he loves to make last-minute decisions, I think I should do the same. Leave him to me," Lyla told her, and the office applauded. "Ladies," she said to the two women behind the reception desk, "if you would start this celebration..." She motioned towards the speakers.

Orla beamed. "With pleasure." The harsh office lights were dimmed and the music, which was usually soft classical tones to appease clients, began pounding out the Christmas classic 'Rockin' Around the Christmas Tree'. Once the champagne was popped, it wasn't long before the dancing began. Lyla hadn't known that Fergus from accounting had such rhythm beneath his tweed jacket. She would never look at him the same again.

Sam joined her at the edge of the crowd and handed her a glass of champagne.

"I can feel a storm brewing," he said, as Lyla watched everyone let their hair down.

"Don't take life so seriously. What can Klaus do? Fire everyone?" She grinned, downing the champagne. Before he could reply, she handed him another glass from the tray on the reception desk. "Drink and be merry!"

"Cheers," he said, and they clinked glasses before joining the makeshift dancefloor.

Just before midnight, Sam reminded Lyla about Secret Santa.

"Secret Santa will start at midnight!" she announced, raising her glass of champagne to the crowded room of smiling faces. There was a cheer as the clock struck the hour, marking only thirteen days before Christmas. She finished her drink, and Sam helped her off the chair.

"Klaus is going to eat you for Christmas dinner when no one shows up tomorrow," he warned in a gleeful whisper.

"Sam, lighten up. I'll handle everything in the morning. We still saved the money he wanted on the party, so I think he can budge a little." Kicking off her heels, Lyla pushed them under the table by the reception desk where they usually greeted the guests.

"I think the champagne has made you delusional," Sam said, offering her another glass.

"Perhaps." She took a sip. "But again, that's tomorrow's problem. Right now, I have to get the secret Santa presents." Pushing through the crowd, she wondered if others in the building had joined them. The main office seemed a little more packed than usual.

Heading to her office, she spotted a light on down the hall away from the party and frowned. The last thing she needed was Klaus finding a stray sock from some late-night shenanigans as the champagne got the better of the staff. It wouldn't be the first time the offices had been used for meaningless flings after one of their legendary parties. She wasn't one to judge, but not in *his* office! He would notice if a pen was so much as put back in the wrong pot.

She grabbed the red sack of presents from under her desk and hurried back to the party, thrusting it at Sam. "Get started without me," she yelled over the music, but he was already looking for his name in the pile.

Slowly, so as not to startle the couple, she padded back down the corridor, the cold marble reminding her she still wasn't wearing shoes. Reaching the door with light shining from underneath it, she listened for a moment and then gave a quiet knock to warn anyone in a state of undress of her presence. No one answered.

"Please re-join the party," she called. "We're about to start with the secret Santa presents—" She pushed open the door with an unintentionally dramatic swing – *the champagne must have hit me harder than I thought* – and then stumbled back.

Mason Klaus was sitting at his desk with his head in his hands. His hair, which was usually groomed to perfection, fell through his fingers, the length concealing his face.

Lyla closed the door behind her, wondering if he was angry about the party. She didn't want to be scolded in front of her co-workers.

"Okay, before you have a go at me for having the party behind your back, I think you should know I paid for it out of my own pocket," she said defensively. When there was no reply, she took a step closer.

"Klaus?" she said gently as she heard heavy breathing.

He looked up, seeming surprised to see her. He hastily smoothed back his hair and went to readjust his tie, but it was already on the desk, his top buttons undone. Lyla couldn't help staring. She had never seen Mr Klaus even slightly out of composure. He looked like a total stranger.

"Is everything alright? You look... distressed." She might not like him, but she was human, and he looked as though he'd been crying – which both saddened and terrified her.

"Lyla – Ms Smurfit – I suggest you go back to your party," he said gruffly, before reaching into his desk drawer and pulling out a decanter she didn't know he had. She didn't know what she was more surprised by – the fact that he'd used her first name in the office for the first time in a year, or that he'd been concealing expensive liquor in his desk drawer.

"Are you going to stand there and stare, or will you join me for a drink?" he asked when she didn't move. It sounded like he might have already indulged in a few.

"I don't think that's a good idea. Why don't I call your car?" she said as he poured another, clinking the decanter hard on the glass. She hadn't seen anyone drink like this since her mother had died. It was how her father had spent most of his nights for the first year. She knew Klaus wouldn't want her to see him like this.

"My car is unavailable," he informed her, "and I couldn't get a cab in the rain. This was the closest place with a couch from the bar." To her horror, he started undoing his shirt buttons, exposing the body he worked so hard on beneath.

"What are you doing? The staff could see and get the wrong impression!" She locked the door before returning to his side and trying to stop him by putting her hand over his. He surprised her by looking at her like *she* was the drink he wanted to indulge in. She quickly let go of his shirt, not wanting him to get the wrong idea.

"Are you trying to take advantage of me, Ms Lyla?" he purred, and she wanted to smack him.

"I'm making sure Sam can't come in looking for me," she snapped. "I'm sure the sober you would never recover from the shame of the staff finding you without a shirt and with me. Alone."

That seemed to sober him a little; he straightened in the chair. Only a few buttons were undone, but he made no move to correct them. Instead, he reached for another drink.

"If you don't want a drink, then go back to the party," he growled, though it sounded like a warning.

"If this is because of that party, then I think you're

overreacting," she shot back, though surely it had to be something else. She needed to get him talking, stop him drinking, and get him out of the office. *I want his position, but not because he ruined his reputation!*

He reached for his jacket, slung over the back of the chair, and a red envelope fell to the floor with words shining up at her in gold cursive.

Mason Klaus, Lyla read, before he picked it up and waved it in front of her. The torn edge told her he had already read its contents.

"Curious, are you?" he said coldly, before tossing it on the desk. "A letter from my family." There was a hint of pain that she recognised in his voice. Her father had had the same undertone when he had told Lyla her mother had passed away.

"A Christmas card? That was nice of them," she tried, but the look she received told her it was anything but. He'd never mentioned his family in all the months they had worked together – not where he was from or what they did. She wasn't ashamed to admit that she'd tried to find him on social media as well as Google, hoping to dig up some dirt on him – know thine enemy and all that – but there was no trace of him. The only thing she could find was his graduation photo and the companies he had worked for. Nothing personal.

"Nice? They're trying to strangle the life from me!" He reached for the glass, but she lunged for it, pushing it out of his reach. Furious, he rose from the chair; she was pressed against the desk, his hands on either side of her. He looked like he was about to tear her apart, if her racing heart didn't do it first.

"I don't think you've much life to strangle," she mumbled, trying to ease the tension. With her heels off, he towered over her. His eyes studied every inch of her expression, and she felt herself cowering as he focused on her lips. She leaned away.

"Maybe not, but it's mine," he muttered.

As suddenly as he'd risen, Klaus softened his gaze and waved a hand in silent apology before reclaiming his seat. Lyla clutched the empty glass to her chest, and once there was enough space for her to slip out from between him and the desk, she placed it back on the desk, slightly out of his reach.

"I don't want you to smell of whiskey in front of the staff," she admitted.

"It's a party, isn't it?" He once again reached for an imaginary tie – *must be a nervous tick.*

"Yes," she admitted, looking at the closed door as they heard laughter from the other side, "but you aren't *at* the party."

He huffed, eyeing the decanter in front of him. *Would he drink it straight from the bottle?* She took it before he could and poured herself a drink. Klaus rubbed his jaw, watching her expression as the amber liquid burned the back of her throat. She winced. As more of a gin lover, the whiskey burn was unfamiliar.

"Are you going home for the holidays? Christmas can be a tense time for many families..." She wondered why she hadn't left him to his whiskey. After a moment of being ignored, she decided to do just that. She tipped back the glass to finish it.

"My father is dead, and I haven't been home in years." The harsh words were spoken devoid of any emotion.

Lyla choked on the whiskey, her eyes watering. He merely raised his eyebrows as she patted her chest and tried to soothe the ache.

"I'm so sorry," she managed to say, putting down the glass and sitting on the chair opposite him. *He hasn't seen his family in years?* She couldn't imagine not seeing her dad for so long. *Something must have happened to keep them apart.*

"My sister wrote the letter. The one who hates to write. I haven't spoken to them in – ten years? Ten? Has it been that long? Kev will be..." He stared into the distance in disbelief, as if he'd forgotten she was there.

"An invitation to the funeral?" she asked softly.

"No. There was no need," Mason said firmly. He didn't elaborate.

"Okay..." *No need for a funeral? Or no need for an invitation to it?* The latter made more sense, but she couldn't exactly pry when they weren't even on a first-name basis, or hadn't been until about ten minutes ago.

He slumped back in his chair with a groan. "I have to go home. Less than two weeks before Christmas – they'll be out of their minds with work..." He tailed off into a sleepy mumble. *That'll be the whiskey kicking in.*

Lyla couldn't take it a moment longer. She was getting him out of here. She reached into her skirt pocket for her phone and texted Sam.

> Had to leave. Make sure everyone leaves safely. My spare keys are in my desk, give them to security when you're last to leave. L 😘

She didn't like leaving the office without making sure everyone had gone first, but she trusted her colleagues not to destroy the place.

"Where are your house keys?" she asked Klaus, who shrugged with a tipsy smile.

"That's not helpful," she muttered, checking his desk and finding nothing. She considered reaching into his pockets, but didn't want to face the embarrassment of it tomorrow. She eventually found them in his discarded jacket, much to her relief. The private lift to the executive car park below would be her saviour: she could spare dragging him out in front of everyone.

"A taxi it is," she announced, remembering he had no car. While they waited for the lift, she called parking security to have them arrange one.

Mason smiled as she placed an arm around him and helped him walk unsteadily to the lift. The doors opened and they stepped in.

"You have no shoes on," he pointed out. "How irresponsible of you."

Lyla stared at her feet, annoyed at herself. She could ask Sam to bring them to her, but then he'd see Mr Klaus, and her assistant loved to gossip more than anyone.

"And you're drunk off two glasses of whiskey – who's more of an embarrassment?" she rebutted.

He leaned against the side of the lift. "I wish it was only two. I have to go home."

"It might be nice to spend Christmas with your family. With a loss, they would miss you otherwise."

"Stop talking! I meant I have to get back to my house."

Lyla zipped her lips about his Christmas plans. Suddenly, he was leaning less against the wall and more on her shoulder. She was relieved she wasn't wearing her heels, or she would have toppled over. They staggered out, and she was too busy trying to get him to walk across the car park in a straight line to listen to him mumbling something about fate catching up with him.

"Tell the nice man your address," she said, opening the

waiting taxi door and shoving him less-than-gently inside. Despite what society thought of her slightly-too-curvy-to-be-acceptable figure, she was pretty strong, but she still couldn't support him. Much to her relief, Mr Klaus snapped to attention as he hit the leather back seat and called out the address in a burst.

"Sorry, Miss, but you can't leave him in this state," the taxi driver told Lyla.

"What? You can't be serious!"

The driver looked unbothered by her distress. "If he gets sick, I ain't cleaning it. He's in no state to pay a fine or give his details if he does."

Mason was already half-asleep in the backseat. Lyla bit her lip. She knew the driver was right, but she was barefoot, freezing cold, and only had her phone. "I need to pop back upstairs to grab my shoes—"

"Sorry, love, can't be waiting this close to Christmas. I already have two fares lined up after this."

This late and so close to Christmas, it would be nearly impossible to find another taxi at this time. *Maybe I should go with him and head home from there. He might need help getting inside.* The taxi driver certainly wasn't going to help – not that she could blame him. It wasn't his job to look after drunk people, but it didn't mean she wanted to either. She told herself to lord this event over Klaus for the foreseeable future, only to be reminded by the letter sticking out of his pocket that his father had just died. Guilt forced her into the back of the car.

To her disgust, Klaus rested his head on her shoulder. The only bright spot was that her feet were now off the ice-cold cement.

"Fine. Two stops. His first," Lyla said. "Embassy Avenue, number 96." Luckily, she could pay for this with her phone, but she wished she hadn't left her shoes and bag upstairs. She had a hideaway key so she could get into her house, but she didn't like being barefoot.

"She has no shoes," Mason told the driver, who frowned in the mirror.

"Ignore him," Lyla said, giving the driver a reassuring nod. The last thing she needed was Klaus causing trouble with his rambling during the drive.

The security guard opened the gate, letting them out.

CHAPTER THREE

While Lyla lived in the townhouse her mother had left her, which had once been her art studio, Mason lived in a restored Victorian building that had once been an embassy. The immaculately kept street was rife with embassies; you couldn't step outside the door without seeing a Range Rover and a security detail. Lyla wondered if Klaus was worried about his personal safety, since he'd apparently chosen the safest street in the country to live on. The taxi pulled up to the curb, and she opened the door.

"How long are you going to be?" the taxi driver grumbled. "I have places to get to."

"If you wait, I'll cover your next two fares," she told him, and he looked to the meter.

"Next four," he bargained.

Lyla looked at her bare feet, unsure another taxi would

take her without shoes. She didn't want to wait on the street in the middle of the night, no matter how safe the street.

"Deal." She helped Klaus out of the car. "Mind the step," she scolded, struggling to open the front gate, which stupidly had a ledge. By the time they reached the front door she was exhausted, and he was trying to catch the falling snow in his hand. He might be enjoying the snow, but she was freezing without a jacket or shoes.

"Keys?" she half-begged, only to receive a shrug. Giving up, she reached inside his jacket and took them. Klaus leant against the door while she twisted the key in the lock. Lights turned on automatically, revealing a home she would envy for the rest of her days. The carpeted hallway was a warm welcome to her feet, but he was still lingering in the doorway, watching her.

"Want to sleep on the stoop?" she demanded. He was letting the warm air escape.

"Can't you be a little gentler?" he grumbled. "I thought a drink would remove some of your thorns!"

Ignoring that, Lyla led him through the house. A sitting area shared the open plan space with a library full of more books than she could count. Out the back was a kitchen she never wanted to have to figure out how to use. A winding staircase by the library wall seemed to be the only way up to the second floor. She eyed it suspiciously. Klaus took a step towards it, but she could already picture the headlines: *Smurfit partner found dead after drunken tumble down stairs.* Everyone in the office knew how much they loathed each other; she'd be convicted of his murder. There was no way she was getting him up those.

"How can you not have a Christmas tree?" she panted. There wasn't a single Christmas decoration through the house.

"I'm sick of Christmas. The whole city, even my office window, is infected with the sight of that giant tree. This is one place Christmas can't corrupt," he said, swaying on his feet, though it was the clearest thing he'd uttered since leaving the office. Seeing the rising flush of anger on his cheeks, Lyla instantly knew better than to ask any more questions.

"Bed?" she asked. He collided with her as he tried to slip off his shoes.

"Why? Want to join me?" A lazy smile lit up his features.

She couldn't help but smirk at the hedgehogs on his black socks. *Maybe he isn't as dead inside as he likes others to believe.*

"In your dreams," she snarked, and he laughed – a half-hearted, almost pained laugh. He straightened up a little too quickly and began to fall, making her dart forward to catch him. With his body pressed against hers, she could practically count how many hours he'd spent working out. She moved her hand from his abdomen to his chest as he swayed forward dangerously, and his hand covered hers. A shiver ran through her. She told herself it was just the chill until she glanced up at him to find his eyes searching hers.

"Have your eyes always been so amber?" he asked, leaning down towards her. She snatched her hand away as his expression told her he was thirsty for something other than water.

"Yes." His frown told her he'd already forgotten his question. "The couch is the best we can do," she decided, leading him towards the area with a huge TV and a plush carpet that was heaven on her bare feet. She pushed him back onto the couch. He grabbed a pillow and shoved it under his head, making himself comfortable. With a glass front to the house, she considered turning on the heating, but didn't know how or where she could turn it on. Instead she went to the kitchen and found a glass for water.

By the time she returned, he was shirtless and sprawled on his back, obviously not caring that she was there. She placed the glass on the table beside him so he wouldn't have to go far. Not knowing where to look – and ignoring the voice in her head that told her exactly where to – she plucked a thin blanket from the armchair by the fire and threw it over him. *Only someone so hateful could look so tempting. Typical – the only time I'm attracted to him, and he's unconscious. If only his mouth didn't have to ruin it.* He always questioned her decisions, he could never trust her judgement. Even when ordering office supplies, he insisted on black pens instead of blue, because they were two percent cheaper. She loathed being micro-managed.

She looked at his lips, wondering how much damage they could truly do. Another shiver shot through her, and she hastily turned to the electric fireplace. She had no idea how to start it; her own only needed wood and a spark. There were no other blankets she could see, and she looked over his half-naked state, knowing he'd feel the cold once the drink wore off. She rocked on her heels, wondering if she should go up the stairs. The cold metal steps were a far cry from the carpet, but she found his bedroom; upstairs looked like an unloved showroom compared to the welcoming library and living space downstairs. She pulled the thick cream blanket from the end of his bed, looking around. Piles of books on finance, politics and nothing she would have considered bedtime reading littered the floor. There was a photo on the bedside table.

"One photo?" she asked herself, picking up the intricate gold frame. A family all sitting in a traditional Santa sleigh smiled up at her. On closer inspection, she spotted Klaus, who appeared to be in his early teens. Behind them, there seemed to be a Christmas festival happening.

"They might have taken him to loads of Christmas events and he got sick of them?" she wondered aloud, running her hand over the happy picture. Klaus was smiling too, something she hadn't seen often, and certainly not like this. *Come to think of it, tonight was probably the first time I've seen him actually smile – but that doesn't count anyway, since it was triggered by half a bottle of whiskey and lord knows what else before I got to him.*

With the blanket tucked under her arm, Lyla placed the photo back where she'd found it. His home screamed privacy, and she doubted he'd appreciate her looking at the one personal item he displayed.

Downstairs, she covered him with the heavy blanket. She thought about leaving him a note, in case he didn't remember how he'd got home. Then again, she doubted he would want to remember any of this night. Picking up the discarded suit jacket, the gleaming envelope in his pocket caught her eye. She glanced at him; he was sleeping peacefully. Unable to stop herself, she pulled it out.

She barely had the letter out of the envelope before a hand shot out, causing her to jump out of her skin. Lyla started to apologise, only to find that Klaus was still sleeping. *One day my curiosity will kill me.* With a sigh of relief, she tucked the letter back in his pocket.

Standing by the door, she suddenly felt wrong leaving him. Thinking of the grief so fresh in his heart, and how he was apparently estranged from his family, she wondered if she should stay. Then she reminded herself that even drunk, he had only opened up an inch. By the morning, she would only be an intrusion she doubted he'd want to worry about. *It's better to respect his pain instead of satisfying my own need to make it better.*

She decided to pretend this night had never happened, and closed the door behind her.

CHAPTER FOUR

Lyla vowed a painful death to whoever was pounding on the door before seven. It was probably her neighbour coming to rant about her cat, Jones, being in their garden. She snuggled her pillow closer to her head, hoping to drown out the sound. It wasn't her fault they insisted on having bird feeders; *how was Jones supposed to control himself when given the perfect opportunity to play?* Her neighbour usually gave up after a few minutes, but the banging continued, followed by the doorbell chiming to the tune of Jingle Bells in quick succession. She was ready to kill as she grabbed a clip to restrain her morning curls and stumbled out of bed, the champagne hangover adding to her rage.

"JONES!" she roared as her chunky ginger cat scrambled between her feet, causing her to trip. He scampered away. The banging at the door seemed to get louder the longer she delayed. She yanked on her dressing gown as Jingle Bells continued to chime.

"What in the Scrooge is wrong with you?" Lyla snapped, turning the key in the door – to see a sober and no-less-than-perfect Mr. Klaus.

For a moment she stared at him blankly, her mind scrambling to figure out why he was standing on her doorstep at the crack of dawn. *This is how he thanks me for saving his drunken arse?* The collar of his long coat was pulled up to protect him from the falling snow.

"Good morning, and goodbye!" She attempted to close the door in his face and leave him to freeze, but his hand gripped the frame.

Nice reflexes, she thought, then was disgusted at herself for being impressed. Her hungover mind drifted to him shirtless on the couch last night, and she was impressed for an entirely different reason.

He cleared his throat, returning her to the present moment. He was holding a phone up for her to see.

"I need my contacts," she told him, seeing a blurry video playing.

Instead of letting her go, he thrust the phone closer. *What the hell could be so important?!* Lyla took the phone from him. She held it a little too close to her face, and waited for her eyes to focus.

"Watch the video, Lyla," Klaus ordered, his voice dripping with venom. She didn't like the way her name sounded in that tone. Usually, he referred to her as Ms Smurfit. If he left the door open any longer, she would be as blue as a Smurf. She wanted him gone; maybe reminding him of his embarrassing state yesterday would persuade him to leave.

"Aren't you hungover? How can you be here when you could hardly stand last night?"

Klaus ignored her, and she reluctantly focused on the screen again. She watched the camera pan over what looked like the office – except the Christmas tree was on its side, surrounded by broken ornaments. The lounge was covered in tinsel and wrapping paper, with more than a few broken bottles littering the floor. She was about to argue that the damage wasn't too bad when the video moved through to the staff kitchen, which was cloaked in smoke. As blackened walls and two firefighters came into view, she lost the ability to think.

"There was a fire?" she demanded frantically. "Was anyone injured?"

Mr Klaus made his way into the hall and closed the door behind him, stopping the snow from following him in.

"No, thankfully. Only my pride, and your reputation." He seemed to lose his composure. "Your scheme could have burnt down the building. We aren't the only ones who occupy the high rise!"

She was taken aback. It was the first time he raised his voice at her. They had fought plenty of times, but he'd always been able to get his infuriating points across without raising his voice a decibel.

"Is this what you had in mind for a Christmas party?" he hissed, his cheeks flushed. "When I arrived this morning, there were firefighters coming and going from the lobby. Someone thought it was a good idea to reheat a pizza in the toaster." His eyes were also reddened, presumably by the hangover.

"I told Sam to make sure everyone got out," she said pathetically.

"They got out, but they left their pizza burning. I don't like waking up to the fire department telling me our office is riddled with black smoke and a burnt-out kitchen!" The last few words seemed to further his anger, and he ran a hand through his hair, which was haphazardly tied at the back of his neck.

"I'm not entirely to blame for this! It wouldn't have happened if I hadn't had to bring your drunken self home!" she flared up at him, only to falter when she realised that it probably *was* her fault for one, leaving the party, and two, throwing it in the first place.

He closed his eyes and pinched the bridge of his nose. "I need coffee and painkillers if we are to continue this conversation," he breathed, and pushed past her like it was his own home. "This is why you need me to run the company. Because you can't take responsibility for your actions," he added over his shoulder.

He was wrong about the company, but he was right about last night. It was her fault. Guilt made her stomach twist and tumble.

He opened a door off the hallway, and before she could stop him, he was in her sitting room. Lyla fidgeted with the sleeves of her pink robe as he took in the decor with a concerned frown.

"You really are obsessed with Christmas," he said, looking at the decorated fireplace with gold tinsel and stockings. "Did you paint your walls to match your tree?"

"Green is my favourite colour, and yes, it just so happens to match my tree," she admitted, looking at the dark forest-green walls. The Christmas tree was much too big for the room, and her ornaments were displayed with pride on every surface: everything from ceramic reindeer to snow globes. "I like Christmas – sue me." She folded her arms over her chest, trying to warm herself; he had let in the cold, and she only wore her oversized Rudolph T-shirt beneath her thin robe.

"There is a fine line between like and obsession, but at least there is treatment you can seek," he said dryly, picking up the mug on her counter shaped like a Santa hat. She snatched it from him and placed it back on the table before he tainted it with his Scrooge-ness.

"Therapy is normal, and after your reaction to your sister's letter last night, I should book you a session." She was half serious. She'd been in therapy ever since she'd lost her mum in a car accident. She had struggled to get into a car for years, and though she had now come to peace with that, she hadn't mastered driving.

"I didn't mean any offence. I've never met anyone with so many..." Klaus went to the sofa, picked up a candy-cane-shaped pillow and waved it.

"Can we focus less on my decor and more on what to do about the office?"

"It's already taken care of; I have a friend who is an architect. She has a team of builders already seeing to the structural damage."

"Great. I want to meet her!"

"There's no rush. Seems you got your wish after all." His words sounded like an accusation.

"My wish?" Lyla spotted Jones staring at Klaus from a crouched position. She silently hoped the cat would pounce on him and ruin his immaculately tailored suit.

"We have to close the offices until after Christmas because of the smoke damage. She'll be able to get started on the remodel over the season. Some people don't mind working over the holidays."

She wondered if he was afraid the Christmas spirit in her home was contagious.

"If you have everything under control, and I mean this with utter sincerity, *why* are you banging on my door at..."

She looked at the antique clock on her mantle. "SIX AM! Are you insane?" She flopped on the couch. Jones hopped up beside her and took a defensive position on her lap. She appreciated the support, but if he was sitting with her, he couldn't attack Klaus.

"I woke up at four thanks to a call from the fire department. I thought it only fair I disturb the culprit," he informed her. "I thought you would be pleased to hear. The staff have been notified of their twelve days off being restored." He seemed more upset by that than their building nearly being burnt to the ground.

"You didn't by any chance bang your head last night? I don't think the company insurance covers such drastic changes in personality. If you have everything under control, then please – leave."

He was pacing slowly by the fireplace. "Funny. My sister will like you. However, I'm not done yet. We have one more matter to deal with."

She wasn't sure if she had heard him correctly. "Your sister?"

He shook his head. "Never mind. We'll return to work after New Year's, but we'll have to work from home. We can't greet clients in a construction site."

He is actually giving everyone a holiday. That's uncommonly courteous of him. Has his own sudden loss caused him to see that people need time with their families? Or... wait. Is he only doing this because now he has to go home for the holidays? He doesn't have to go; he could stay home and pretend he never got the letter. Then again, she knew he was a stickler for duty. *Maybe he* does *have a conscience and won't let his family grieve without him.*

"I'm sure the clients and staff will appreciate it. I'll speak to Sam about what happened." She couldn't shift the weight of responsibility she felt for the destruction. She had never thought the staff would do something so irresponsible – but then she remembered the crates of champagne. *With that much alcohol, anything is possible.*

"Since you've got what you wanted, and made my offices inhospitable in the process," Klaus went on, "you owe me." Lyla didn't like the glint in his eye.

"*Our* offices," she reminded him, "and I knew it was too good to be true. A leopard can't change its stripes."

He winced. "It's spots. Anyway, I told you not to go ahead with the party, and you did, resulting in a fire that's going to take a sizeable chunk out of our next budget. If we look at our contracts, you could lose your shares for such an action."

"I paid for the party out of my own pocket, and the fire wasn't my fault. I was with you when it was started!"

"You might have paid for the party, but I'll have to pay for the construction. The company is low on capital, and the insurance won't cover due to the cause." He said it patiently, but she noticed that he rubbed his brow as if this conversation was taking a lot out of him. Lyla closed her eyes. Her own head was pounding, and she could see that he was right.

"Okay. Fine. I would rather see the back of you. What do you want? Me to work overtime? I'll happily fill in and sacrifice my Christmas season if it means removing the stick from your—"

"I need you to come home with me for the holidays."

From his blank expression, he wasn't kidding.

"Home with you? You *must* have hit your head when I left you." She placed her head in her hands.

Jones started pawing at her, clearly looking for his breakfast. She stroked the ears of the ginger cat and headed for the kitchen.

"Not that I can recall – but I did wake up half-naked... and since my shirt and jacket were folded, I think you were there for that part." He followed her past the old creaky staircase and into the lime-green kitchen; she could practically feel his grin boring into her back.

"I'm going to ignore that. Removing your clothes was your own work." She sat Jones on his tower and went to the cupboard for the food, feeling Klaus watching her. She couldn't stand the silence. "Why would you even want me to go home with you? We can't be in the same room without killing each other."

"I need a buffer between me and my family – someone without emotional complications. My father's workshop will need to be organised; the family's already overworked with the season. I have no choice, I can't pretend my sister didn't reach out," he told her while she placed some dried food in Jones's bowl.

"You're serious." Lyla searched his cold, dark eyes for any deception, but there wasn't any hesitation in his response.

"Yes."

"I can't—"

"Why not?" he reasoned. "Mr Smurfit is on his honeymoon – the week in Bali *I* gifted him. I'm sure your friends would understand if something pressing comes up..."

Bali was his idea? How can he be so nice to my dad and so incorrigible in my company?

"I have plans with Sam and his husband," she informed him. "I'm supposed to go to them for Christmas dinner. I have a marathon of movies to watch, and most importantly, I plan not to be around you."

He scowled at her. "You see him every day at work, and they have each other. I'm sure they wouldn't mind having a Christmas alone together."

She delighted in the fact that he sounded slightly desperate. "Say please. Say, 'Please, Lyla! I *need* you to come home with me for the holidays'."

He looked away from her and groaned. "Lyla, will you please come home with me for Christmas?"

"Say I need you," she pressed, folding her arms.

"I need you," he ground out, but once the words were out there was a sorrow in his eyes.

"Would it really be so hard to go back alone?"

"I said what you wanted – are you coming or not?" he asked impatiently.

She was horrified to realise that she was actually considering it. *I wanted someone to face my first Christmas without Mum. And if he's estranged from his family and so worried about their business, maybe I* could *help... It could be my charity work for the year...* He shifted nervously as she thought.

"Fine – since you begged," she said at last. "The party is my mess. I'll help you, but we go as friends."

Some colour returned to his cheeks. "It's only until the 26th. I promise you'll be back in Dublin after that, and we'll never have to discuss it again. We'll return as though nothing happened."

Jones rubbed against Klaus' legs. Lyla had never seen him take to anyone that quickly. *Traitor.*

"Do I need to book flights? How far away is your family?" Most flights would be fully booked by now.

"Far," Mason said shortly, fidgeting with his tie.

"I can hire a car, but you'll have to drive and tell me how long the journey is." Lyla was already thinking of what she should pack. Jones tried to climb Klaus's leg, and she quickly scooped the cat up before his nails tore a hole in his navy suit. She didn't need to owe him another favour.

"A car will only take us so far; the village is protected."

Klaus closed the distance between them, reminding her that she was still only in her shorts and top. *Protected? What's that supposed to mean?* She would have asked, but under his gaze she felt rather exposed. Before she could step back, he reached into his pocket and pull out a round gold bell which fitted neatly in the palm of his hand.

"This should do the trick. No need to worry about arrangements," he told her, tossing it and catching it again. She noted his sad smile as he looked at the bell. *Does he think this is a car key? Maybe he really did hit his head.*

"I think we should take you in for a scan. Let me get dressed and I'll take you," she tried to persuade him, but Klaus didn't budge. Lyla stared up at him.

He hesitated, and then wrapped an arm around her waist. With Jones occupying her arms, she couldn't push him away.

"Hey! I don't like whatever game you're playing—"

The soft chimes of the bell echoed around the kitchen. The walls faded around her as if the walls were melting. In a panic, Lyla clutched Jones tight and leant into Klaus's embrace, eyes squeezed shut, afraid she would fall through the floor.

CHAPTER FIVE

The chiming stopped as quickly as it had begun. Lyla heard the crunch of snow underfoot and sharp cold cut through her, causing her eyes to snap open. She shoved herself away from Klaus and clutched Jones tight to her chest, trying to warm herself. They were standing in the middle of a snowy foreign street, the wind threatening to turn her to ice. She wrapped her arms around herself, trying to protect her body as much as she could from the harsh climate. *This is not the weather for pyjamas!*

"This is a d-dream! B-bells don't bring p-people p-places," she stammered, stepping away from the snow-bank and onto a cobble path carved free of snow to save her bare feet.

"Take a few breaths. Travelling by bell can be unsettling on the nervous system," Klaus said, removing his jacket. He tried to wrap it around her, but she backed away.

"Stay away from me, and explain!" she demanded, only to slip on an icy cobble and land in the bank of snow. When the cold didn't wake her from what *had* to be a dream, she clutched the snow in her hands, discovering that it felt very real.

Jones played with the falling snow while Klaus helped Lyla to her feet. She was about to demand answers again when a family in a sleigh pulled by a reindeer passed them with a polite wave – and some concerned glances at her attire.

"I definitely hit my head," Lyla said.

Klaus pulled the jacket around her. "Don't worry; you're perfectly safe here. You can trust me," he told her, his hands on the collar of the jacket.

She wanted to believe him, and once the jacket was belted, she felt a little more secure. "Trust you or not, where are we?" Afraid of losing him in a strange place, she picked up Jones, who protested a little before settling in her arms again.

"Showing is much easier than telling," said Klaus, turning her around.

She was greeted by a flurry of golden lights. The sight of the vast village transfixed her so much that she forgot the burning cold settling in her legs. The whole village looked like a Christmas advert. The logged buildings were covered in fairylights, and the doors were marked with wreaths. Snow-covered mountains surrounded them. *Was that what he had meant when he said the village was protected?* She realised she was crushing Jones.

"Welcome to Yule, or as you might know it, the North Pole," he said.

"Yule. The North Pole." Lyla couldn't believe what she was saying. She was too stunned to protest as Klaus took her hand and led her to the entrance of the village, where she read a wood-carved sign. *Village of Yule. Population 20,000. Established 270AD.* The letters were in the same gold cursive she'd noticed on the letter he'd received.

"Why are you not wearing any shoes?" Klaus asked with a frown.

"Are you the dumbest person in the world? You didn't bother to let me get changed! My *feet* are what you're concerned about? I'm in my pyjamas in the middle of a village that looks like Christmas threw up on it!" Lyla pointed out, trying not to sound hysterical. His lack of reaction was infuriating.

"I can't bring you home with frostbitten toes," he mused, before scooping her up in his arms.

"Are you kidding me?! I don't need to be carried like a child!" She struggled, but he only held her closer.

"Yes, you do. Walking through the village without shoes will inspire too much talk."

"And you carrying me won't? And since when do you care what others think?"

They started towards the village, down a street of snow-cleared cobbles.

"Can you please relax? My head is throbbing enough without your squeaking," he groaned.

Lyla was too distracted by the candy-cane lampposts lighting the way to argue. She stared, transfixed, at the beautifully painted shop windows full of toys, clothes and crafts. The smell of hot chocolate and mince pies emanated from a bakery they passed, and her stomach growled, desperate for breakfast. However, the clear starry night above told her that it was already late here.

"I didn't think the village would shock you so much, considering that your own house is like a shrine to the season," Klaus mocked. Lyla would have smacked him if she hadn't been holding on to a curious Jones for dear life. His soft fur was the only thing grounding her in reality.

"How much longer do you have to carry me? If you'd let me get dressed before warping us here, I could have put shoes on!" She wanted to free herself from his arms as people passing them on the streets and came out of the busy shops began to stare at their display, though they lost interest quickly. Lyla noted that everyone looked to be in a great hurry, many carrying wrapped parcels. A few people even flew past them on bikes. Lyla wouldn't have dared to cycle on the icy streets, but judging from their matching beige uniforms and stuffed satchels, they seemed to be delivery workers. Her only relief was that everyone was dressed like it was the 21st century; at least she hadn't time travelled, and she would be able to find something to wear. Anything would do, if it would stop the staring.

"Once we reach the rank, we can take a sleigh." Klaus said it like taking a sleigh was the most rational thing in the world. "I didn't want to give you a chance to change your mind. The bell wasn't supposed to take us to town, but magic can be unpredictable." He tossed her in his arms to adjust his grip on her, and she grunted as he tried to pull her in closer.

"Magic? *You* believe in magic?" She laughed, and he tossed her again. The fear of being dropped silenced her.

"Magic, energy – whatever you want to call it. I don't know what's so funny."

A couple stopped to stare at them, whispering to each other.

"And you thought they wouldn't gossip," she snarked.

"Oh, I knew they would gossip about my return, but I'd rather they think I'm lovingly carrying you through the village than dragging a shoeless woman through the snow," he explained.

Lyla doubted they were judging *him.* "You really are the master of perception," she grumbled, burying her face in his shoulder, ashamed of being seen in such a state of disarray. In a small town, word was sure to spread.

"Comes with practice," he said arrogantly.

She gritted her teeth and tried to distract herself from her anger by getting answers. "You're from here? From the heart of Christmas itself?" *Christmas can't be a place, can it?* The bewilderment only furthered her pounding head.

"Born and raised," was all he said.

"Can we go into a shop, so I can get some clothes at least?" Lyla begged.

A group of elderly people came out of a restaurant singing Christmas carols, but in a language she didn't recognise. The tune was familiar from when her parents used to take her to church. Dad had stopped going after Mum's accident, and she couldn't blame him for his loss of faith.

"No, most will be closing now, and I don't have the right coin. I can find something once we reach the house. The rank is at the end of the alley," Klaus said.

The right coin? Must have their own currency. Not like I have my purse anyway. Or my phone!

They reached a set of stairs, and she was forced to snuggle even closer to his chest, terrified he would drop her on the ice-covered steps. His dress shoes weren't exactly made for ice and snow, yet he didn't stumble or sway.

"Are you going to talk to me? Or are you going to keep giving me the barest of information for the remainder of the twelve days?" Lyla asked, watching him curiously. She realised he was nodding. *No – he's greeting everyone we pass. Who the hell is this guy?* Jones squirmed in her arms, and she struggled to hold him.

"Since the village is intent on watching our every move, and since you are an outsider, it's better to wait for explanations until we reach the house." He kept his voice low, which she guessed meant he didn't want anyone to hear. "I'm trying to get to the sleigh rank without anyone stopping us. Once they start talking, you really will think you are dreaming, and I don't need you running off with no shoes and a damn cat."

They reached a lamppost marked with green candy-cane stripes as opposed to the red on the rest, and Klaus dumped her back on her feet.

"I can't run – sure, where would I go? I don't even know where I am," Lyla muttered, trying to use Jones to warm herself. The cold was already eating into her bones. She'd never thought she'd see the day where she longed to be held in Mr Klaus's arms. *Nor did I think I'd be trapped in a winter wonder land which I travelled to by bell.*

Klaus held out his hand as a small sleigh pulled by a reindeer came down the laneway. The animal grunted as it was reined to a stop.

"As I live and breathe! I don't believe my own eyes. Mason? Is that you?" the older driver said delightedly.

"It's been a long time," Klaus said, handing the driver a coin which didn't look like any euro Lyla had seen. She didn't have time to inquire before he pushed her into the back and pulled a fur blanket over her lap. As a rule, she was extremely opposed to the use of real fur, which it seemed this was – but her numb hands and legs demanded warmth, and with the snow falling faster, she would freeze without it.

"A long time? Sure, it must be the guts of a decade. Your return will certainly brighten up the village," the driver continued.

"Just a visit, Argyle. If we could get going? We're in a bit of a hurry," Klaus said kindly, and the driver waved a hand.

"Say no more. Where to, Mr Klaus?"

"The Klaus Cabin, please."

The driver snapped the reins, the force pushing Lyla back into the sleigh. If she hadn't been holding Jones, she would have pinched herself. *Riding in a sleigh in the North Pole – how did my life come to this?*

"Do your family live in the cabin, or is it yours?" she whispered, not wanting to be heard by the driver.

"The whole family have lived there since the village came to fruition." Klaus folded his arms over his chest; she wasn't sure if he was cold or being defensive. *Came to fruition? What the hell does that even mean?*

"I think the hangover is making me hallucinate," she said when they turned down a Main Street that looked like Christmas had exploded. There was a decorated tree so tall that she tried to get a better look, but the sleigh took off in a different direction.

"I wanted to see the tree," she sighed under her breath.

"If you've seen one, you've seen them all," said Klaus dryly. The sleigh climbed through rows of trees until they could see the village below them in the distance.

"How can you come from such a place and be such a...?" Lyla breathed into her hands, stopping herself. She was about to meet his family, and she didn't want to be mid-argument when they arrived at the cabin.

"Such a what?" Mason said, leaning in, daring her to continue.

She rose to the challenge. "A Scrooge. People would pay millions to see such a place – hell, even to use that damn bell."

He relaxed back. "No one can ever know you were here, or how we got here. I'm breaking every law there is by bringing you home."

"Then why bring me? If we're breaking the law, why bring more trouble on yourself?" she mumbled, wondering why he was intent on making her the enemy when *he* had brought her here without any warning.

"Because I couldn't return alone," he said, low enough that she barely heard. She didn't say anything else. She knew loneliness was a powerful motivator, and she figured a person couldn't be more alone than Klaus.

The sleigh bolted right for a steep snow path lined with huge uncut trees, the way marked with lampposts. Up the hill, they were high enough to look over the entire village when the trees cleared. The lights called to Lyla; she had never seen anything so pretty. She realised that all the streets and alleys at this height shaped the village into a perfect star, with the huge Christmas tree exactly in the centre.

"If you lean out any further, you'll fall out, and the woods are unforgiving," Klaus warned, taking her arm.

"How could you ever leave?" she wondered, not taking her eyes off the view.

"I see your young miss can appreciate the splendour of Yule, even if you can't," the driver said. Lyla winced; she hadn't meant to be so loud in her admiration.

"Not now, Argyle," Klaus said, and the driver laughed.

"Your family will be delighted to have you back, as will the village. I don't think we ever expected to see your face again. Certainly not with a missus in your arms, traipsing through the village. There'll be plenty of chatter in the workshops tomorrow," he said, peeking at them over his shoulder – at her.

Lyla blushed fiercely. "Missus? No! I'm not his wife."

The sleigh came to a screeching halt.

"Not his wife?" Argyle gawked, then a deep frown darkened his features. Lyla wondered if they really had travelled back in time. *Is not being married a crime?* "The council will want to have a word with you," Argyle told Klaus, who leant forward and patted the elderly man's shoulder.

"Please, Argyle, it's cold, and we have a long evening ahead. All will be explained in time," he said. It seemed to put the man at ease – mostly.

"The council won't be happy about this," he warned. "The village has had enough of a shock with the loss of your father."

Lyla's gut was telling her that this wonderland might not be so wondrous. *Would they truly be so angry that I'm here with him?*

"When have I ever made the council happy?" Klaus said. Argyle looked like he was about to argue his point further, but Klaus interrupted him before he could. "I'm only teasing you. Has age ruined your sense of humour? The village should be rejoicing. I've brought someone home – something else to talk about rather than our loss."

Something to talk about? Is that all I am, just a topic for gossip? Is his relationship with his family and the village really so strained? Lyla didn't know what she was walking into, but judging from Argyle's expression, she might be the one who was unwelcome.

"Cruel as always, sir. You shouldn't joke about tradition. The council certainly won't." Argyle snapped the reigns once again.

Klaus lounged back and gave her a wink but no answers. She scowled at him in response. She needed to speak to him, but clearly there was a part to play that she couldn't keep up with. For her own safety, she opted for silence and enjoyed the view of the village.

CHAPTER SIX

It wasn't long before they reached a set of tall gates with chipped white paint and an emblem in gold cursive at the centre with the letters S and C. The gates opened at their approach. Lyla looked for an electrical cause, but couldn't see one. No camera or sensor visible. No key, electric or otherwise; nothing. *Magic.* The thought scared her more than it should have.

The reindeer led them down a driveway, where a frozen fountain rose in front of the cabin.

Apparently, Lyla's idea of a cabin and Klaus's were vastly different. This one was the size of a manor. It was split into three separate buildings with logged walls, a terrace surrounding the whole lot. They were connected through glass-walled corridors.

"This is not a cabin. *This* is a cabin on steroids," she gasped as the sleigh pulled up to the terrace, where a long walkway led to what seemed to be the main door.

"Have you never seen a house before?" Klaus appeared utterly indifferent.

Lyla shook her head. With Klaus's work ethic, she somehow hadn't expected him to have grown up with a silver spoon. She tried to contain herself, but failed. "A house? The fairy-lights on the terrace, the door marked with two Christmas trees, the giant wreath! This is my heaven!"

"You might not think so once we get inside," he warned, though there was no malice in his voice.

"I'm nervous enough, please let me enjoy this," Lyla pleaded, noticing that the property was crowded with trees and lit by the same lampposts which had guided them here. Beyond them there was only the darkness of coniferous trees and the mountains in the distance. *If Yule is so cut off, how do they get power?*

Full of questions, she turned to ask, but Klaus had already left the sleigh. The double doors of the cabin were flung open. A woman whom Lyla guessed to be in her late sixties, clad in a snowman jumper, hurried down the path extending from a porch towards them.

"Are you getting out? Argyle has his own family to get home to," Klaus said, though he didn't bother to offer her a helping hand.

"Mason! I can't believe you're home," the woman screeched joyfully, coming down the steps at a pace that terrified Lyla. She guessed this was his mother.

"Lyla?" Klaus asked.

"Sorry," she said, stepping reluctantly from the comfort of the furs onto the icy driveway, instantly humiliated to be standing before his approaching mother in his jacket and her pyjamas. She tried to hide behind Klaus, but when the woman wrapped her arms around him, she was exposed.

"Good to see you too, Mum," Klaus said, returning the hug, but with less vigour.

"After all this time, let me take a look at you. So handsome!" His mother stared up at him, only to embrace him once again. "Promise me you won't leave us for so long again. Kevin won't know what to do when he sees you."

Lyla was surprised he didn't combust into flames under all the affection. *There's no anger in her words, not even a stern look. She only looks pleased – elated, even – to see her son. Why was he so nervous about his return?*

"I promise, but can we pause the emotions for a minute? I have someone for you to meet," Klaus said.

His mum, who stood at a fraction of his height, peered around him. "And who might this beauty be?" she said warmly, and Lyla felt a little more at ease.

"Lyla... Smurfit." She didn't know why she'd added her last name. She sounded like she was going for a job interview. Mrs Klaus's eyes were the same striking blue as her son's, though Klaus was missing her friendly disposition.

"Forgive the hysterics. Everything has been a little overwhelming lately." She stopped herself and took a breath. *To lose her husband and regain her son...* no wonder she was overwhelmed. "Here's me prattling on – where are my manners? I'm Mrs Klaus, Mason's mum. You're a sight for sore eyes!" Mrs Klaus exclaimed, taking Lyla's hand. "It's a surprise to see you, but I'm very happy Mason has someone by his side right now. I've hated the thought of him being away and alone all this time."

"Kla—Mason" – she stumbled over his first name; it tasted wrong on her tongue – "keeps himself far too busy to be lonely. I'm sorry for your loss. Please let me be of any use," Lyla offered, and the delight in the woman's smile meant it was the right response.

"Before she can be of use, maybe we should take Lyla out of the cold," Klaus began, but they were interrupted by the slam of a door. A younger boy in his late teens came out with a confused expression and what looked like a half-eaten s'more in his hand. He dropped it, along with his jaw.

He must be Kevin. If Klaus has been gone ten years, he must have only been a kid when he left. I can't imagine having a sibling and not seeing them for so long. Her heart went out to both of them.

"Mum! Come inside – it's freezing!" he called.

Before Lyla could stop him, Klaus walked towards his brother, leaving her alone. She watched as there was a moment's hesitation between the two brothers, now similar in height and stature.

They stared at each other, and then Klaus pulled Kevin into his arms. The younger boy groaned and pulled away, only to smile and return the hug. She would have loved to hear their exchange, but she was too far away.

She remembered that the letter had been written by Klaus's sister. She wondered if she was about to make an appearance too. Lyla might as well be embarrassed in front of the whole Klaus clan.

"Yes, first things first. You poor dear, wearing so little in the mountains, you'll catch your death," Mrs Klaus said, before embracing her and nearly smothering Jones in the process. When Jones mewed in protest, she jumped back in surprise. Lyla brushed his ears to soothe him.

"Kl—Mason didn't exactly give me time to change, or to pack," Lyla informed Mrs Klaus, who was quick to wag a finger at her son in the near distance before returning her attention to the cat. "Sorry – this is Jones. He isn't too good with strangers."

Jones instantly made her a liar by nuzzling into Mrs Klaus' touch while they walked to Klaus by the door.

"He should have let you pack! Mason is always impatient. I see nothing has changed," Mrs Klaus said, smacking her son's shoulder. Even though he towered over the petite and full-figured woman, she clearly wasn't afraid of him or his expression. "He got that scowl from his father."

Klaus rolled his eyes. Lyla didn't know how to respond to the mention of her late husband; for someone grieving, she seemed awfully happy. Then she reminded herself that not everyone grieved the same way. *She's probably just happy to have her son back.*

"It's certainly his trademark – he's famous for it at the company," she said teasingly.

Mrs Klaus took her arm. "You met at work?"

Mason tugged Lyla from his mother's grasp, for which she was grateful. She wasn't sure what their story was, especially if she wasn't supposed to be in Yule.

"Can we save the interrogation for after dinner?" he asked. "As you can see, my fiancée is hardly dressed for the mountains."

Fiancée?! What the fuck? Lyla gave a strangled gasp, and Klaus immediately squeezed her arm almost to the point of pain. She glared up at him, but turned the gasp into a cough. *Whatever reason he has for this lie must be important.*

But when she got him alone she was going to kill him.

"You got engaged?" Kevin said, waiting inside the door.

Too stunned to speak, Lyla gave what she hoped was a polite smile.

"How long have you been engaged?" Mrs Klaus pressed, and Lyla heard the sadness in her voice. The last thing she wanted was to bring her more pain after losing her husband.

"Not long," she managed to croak. *As in thirty bloody seconds! I said I'd come here as a friend – I was trying to be supportive, considerate of his loss. I should have known he would blindside me.*

They walked through the door into a foyer and were greeted by a grand fireplace under a dark wooden staircase.

"You can call me Mum, if you like. Or 'Mrs Klaus', if that would make you more comfortable. No one calls me Edith," she said, with a warm smile.

Mum. Lyla never thought she'd call someone by that title again. She didn't think her voice would let her.

"Thank you, Mrs Klaus. It's nice to finally meet you," she said instead. *We are supposed to be a couple...* Realising she was going along with the lie, she figured the cold must have started to eat away at her brain cells.

Before she knew it, she was being led to the stairs. The bannisters were decorated with ivy and golden tinsel. She knew she should still be furious at Klaus for dropping her into whatever this was, but all she could think about was how she'd suddenly been transported into a fantastical Christmas dreamscape. The decorations were overboard but tasteful, which she hadn't thought was possible.

"Let's get you into a warm bath and some clothes. I can't believe my son brought you to the mountains in so little. One would think he was trying to get you killed," Mrs Klaus teased. Lyla wasn't sure she was altogether wrong.

"I'd love to chat more, but the cold has really got to me," she said apologetically, and Mrs Klaus gave her hand a gentle pat.

"Go and get yourself warm. Breakfast is at seven. Mason can show you to your room upstairs. His room has the best view; I'm sure you'll be comfortable. We'll have plenty of time to get to know each other once you've had a good night's rest," she said. Klaus was already nudging Lyla up the steps. "Oh, and if he's an outside cat, it would be best to keep your furry friend inside. We wouldn't want the wolves to get him."

Wolves? Lyla gave Klaus a frightened look, but he only shrugged as though it were the most normal warning in the world. *I think my dream is quickly becoming a nightmare.*

"Thank you for letting me know. I'll keep him in the room," Lyla said, noticing that Kevin had disappeared without speaking to her. From what she had seen so far, they seemed like a pretty normal family, considering they hadn't seen each other for a long time. She glanced at Klaus, wondering again why he had been so concerned about returning alone when they had received a warm welcome. She would have like to talk to Kevin, but he was a teenager *and* Klaus's brother, so she didn't expect him to hang around and chit-chat.

Then again, once the joy of Klaus's return was extinguished, issues might start to fester.

"I didn't know I'd gain a fiancé in less than twelve hours. A little warning would have been nice," she hissed at Klaus through a false smile once they were out of earshot.

"Just say we're engaged for a few days. Everything will be fine. You'll get to experience a Christmas like never before," he whispered in her ear at the top of the stairs, wrapping an arm round her waist.

She wanted to shove him away, but knew his mother was probably watching. The thought made her want to jump into the fireplace.

"Why?" she demanded as soon as they were out of Mrs Klaus's sight. "Why is me being here a crime?"

"Because you weren't born here, and outsiders aren't supposed to know about the village. They can never know this place truly exists, or it would mean the end of Yule."

"More on that later. If I refuse – if I tell them we aren't a couple – what's the worst they can do?"

He waited to reply until they reached the end of a corridor decorated with soft white carpet and rich red wallpaper, embellished with raised floral details.

"They'll have you killed," he said bluntly.

His words cut through her like glass; she felt the blood drain from her face.

Klaus smirked. "Breathe – I was only messing. Just trying to lighten the mood."

"By saying I could be murdered!" She resisted the urge to strangle him with his stupid tie.

"They won't kill you, but they'd put you on trial, and if you were found guilty they would wipe your memory. A simple tonic, and you'd forget all about this little adventure," he said, as if it wasn't a big deal. When she didn't respond, he continued like he hadn't put her in danger. "The only outsiders who are allowed in Yule are those already wed or engaged to a villager. No one has ever come here without some important bond – not in a couple of hundred years, anyway. The law is a little outdated, but still valid," he said.

Still valid! In the morning, I need to get the hell out of here before they find out the truth. She gripped her hands together to stop them from trembling. The thought of having her memory wiped felt like a gross invasion, and she didn't even want to know about the tonic they used to do it.

Klaus opened the door to the last room on the right. Lyla looked to the other doors along the corridor.

"There are so many rooms – can't I sleep somewhere else?" she asked, feeling her cheeks flush at the idea of sharing with him.

"I think staying in separate rooms would raise questions we don't want answered." He stood in the middle of the room, motioning for her to join him. "I won't bite;

you're safe here," he added, offering her a reassuring smile which did little to ease her worries.

"There is no way I'm sharing a bed with you," she insisted, looking at the welcoming bed in the middle of the room.

"You don't need to worry about sharing the bed. Once my family is asleep, I'll sneak into one of the guest rooms downstairs so I can be close to the office. I'll return before they wake up."

She felt her shoulders relax, knowing she would get some space from him, even if it was only to sleep. "Thank you," she said, knowing he was taking a risk going to another room when he could have taken the couch in the corner.

She examined the far wall, lined with old-fashioned wardrobes. Mason opened one, revealing the suits and smart shoes inside, then quickly moved on to the next. Lyla watched him go through T-shirts and jeans before taking out a plain white jumper and a pair of black joggers, which she guessed were for her. Watching him move from one end of the room to the other was making her dizzy. Everything felt like it was moving too fast. She didn't care about the clothes any more; she cared about answers.

"Can you please stand still for a moment and look at me," Lyla pleaded, putting Jones down on the bed.

Klaus closed the wardrobe and turned to look at her as if she was inconveniencing him.

"I'm all ears, but you really should change," he said, handing her the clothes.

She tossed them on the bed. "You can't be serious about the penalty being a memory wipe. That was just a shock tactic," she said, trying to make sense of the situation. *Klaus... Claus. Is this a joke, as in Santa? There's no way.* As much as she loved Christmas and wanted Saint Nic to be real, she couldn't believe that the ancient being's son had been working down the corridor from her, disguised as the seasonal grouch.

"The laws were written back in a more barbaric time, and it was rare that anyone broke them, so there was never any reason to amend them."

"Marry you or memory loss?" Lyla exclaimed. "I want to go home, right now!"

"You can't – you need to stay." He pointed at the clothes. "Wear these into the village tomorrow. They'll do for now until we get you some that fit," he said, like a parent to a child. She groaned in frustration.

"First the villagers see me in pyjamas, and now in your clothes. They'll think I can't dress myself. How are you expecting anyone to take me seriously?" She followed him to a bathroom which housed an empty tub the size of her kitchen. She fought the urge to turn on the taps and soak her frozen feet.

"I don't care how the villagers see you, as long as they see you as my fiancée." He seemed to care more about rearranging his bath products than talking to her. "Everything you need should be under the sink. Mum must have been keeping my room in order since I left."

The thought of Mrs Klaus maintaining her son's room not knowing whether he would come back was awfully sad, but Lyla didn't have time to dwell on it when her memory was at stake.

"I don't care about toiletries. I can't marry you!"

"Don't flatter yourself. You only need to say we're engaged; we met at the company—"

"I don't know anything about you. We've only known each other a year!" She clenched her fists, willing this nightmare to end.

He shrugged. "My family hasn't seen me in nearly ten years – hasn't heard from me at all. You know where I live, where I work, what I do most days."

"Technically – but I know nothing about you! The only thing I do know is that you dragged me here on false pretences." She remembered his bedroom in Dublin. "And that you like books way too much," she added under her breath.

"Books? How do you know that?"

"Hundreds of them in your house, around your bed, like a madman. Reading is fun and all, but the stacks are excessive."

He rounded the bed and stood over her. "You went up to my bedroom?"

"You are in no position to be annoyed at me!" She rose on her tiptoes, not allowing herself to be intimidated.

"You invaded my privacy."

"You could cost me my memories," she retorted, and his expression softened.

"Only your recent ones." Klaus took her hand, forcing her palm open, and placed in it a simple gold band set with three small diamonds. "Wear this, and no one will doubt us."

She looked down at it. "Where did you get this? When?"

"My drawer. It's been in the family for years."

The thought of wearing a family heirloom made her stomach knot.

"Stop panicking. Act how you usually do with me, and they'll swallow it hook, line and sinker."

She stared at him in confusion. "With utter disdain?"

"Precisely. I spend half my time arguing with them. If I didn't with you, they would know something was wrong," he said, taking the joggers and jumper from the bed. "Now, please change. Your pyjamas are... rather revealing." He raised an eyebrow, admiring her bare legs. She clutched the clothes to her body. The idea of him admiring any part of her made her want to curl up and die of embarrassment.

"I'm leaving in the morning." Lyla shoved past him and slammed the bathroom door, hoping everyone in the house would hear.

"Lyla," he called from the other side. She pressed her back against the door. "I know this is all a shock to you. I didn't plan to bring you here; I shouldn't have." There was a long pause. "Are you listening to me?" he asked softly.

"Yes." She pressed herself closer to the door, wondering if this was the best way for them to have an open and honest conversation. Usually looking at him infuriated her, and today hadn't won him any points. "I'm listening."

"All you have to do is follow my lead, and I'll tell you as much as you need to know to keep you and our secret safe. I'd never let anyone hurt you, regardless of what you think of me."

She processed that. "You won't let them wipe my memory?"

"No, it's an old rule. I doubt they would even enforce it."

"Promise me."

"I promise," he said, and for some reason, she trusted him. He was a man of his word, and though he had concealed his family and his home, he had never actually lied to her. "Will you stay?"

Her gut told her it was a terrible decision. "...Okay."

"I didn't catch that?" he pressed, and she couldn't help the irritation brewing inside her.

"I said okay! But if there's even a hint of danger, I'm leaving," she called out, trying to figure out the many knobs inside the shower.

"Good. Breakfast is at seven am, just in case you forgot."

Was that a jab at my tardiness? Not wanting to get her curls wet, she tied them on top of her head and turned on the shower head.

"Keep the door locked when I'm not here. No one will disturb you. Don't be late," he called through the door, confirming her thought. If the hot water hadn't been bliss on her chilled skin, she'd have thrown open the door and throttled him with the tie on her dressing gown.

"I won't!" she snapped.

She waited, but she didn't hear anything else.

"Fine," she muttered to herself, washing herself with soap that smelt like peppermint. "If he wants a fiancée, then that's exactly what I'll give him. A perfect, doting fiancée." Looking at the ring on her finger, she grinned. "It'll drive him crazy."

CHAPTER SEVEN

When Lyla woke, she had no idea where she was, and even when she remembered, her body didn't know if it was night or day. She never did well with time-zone changes, and she wasn't sure what the time difference between Yule and her home was. Thinking about it made her head hurt, but the clock on the stand beside her read 6:45am, so she'd got a few hours of sleep. The thought of getting more was silenced by her grumbling stomach.

She glared at the men's briefs and clothes Klaus had left out for her, but at least they were better than the robe she'd slept in. She stared at the ring on her finger and groaned in frustration, reminded of all the lies she was about to tell.

Klaus must still be downstairs. Even if she didn't want to share a bed with him, the realisation worried her. *If they find out we aren't engaged, will his family report me to the council Argyle mentioned?*

The jumper and joggers were far too big, so she rolled up the bottoms and cuffed the sleeves. *If I'm going to be here for twelve days, he'll have to take me into the village to get some clothes and the right products for my hair. I think contacts would be pushing it... at least I have my glasses. I might be able to convince his mum or sister to take me once we're better acquainted.*

There wasn't much she could do about her curls, except resecure them in a messy bun. Despite discovering more hair products in the bathroom than anyone should need in their lifetime, Lyla had found nothing to aid her. Her own collection was impressive, though necessary to maintain her curls, but between hair gels and beard oils, he had her beaten. *Then again, maybe Mrs Klaus got them and just wanted to be prepared for anything he might need?* She picked up one of the bottles in bewilderment. *Scented beard oil?* He didn't even *have* a beard. N*o wonder he always looks so perfect; he must get his cosmetic compulsion from his mum.*

She put the bottle back and returned to the bedroom, where she pulled a pair of thick socks on over the long joggers. With little time remaining before she had to go to breakfast, she took a moment to snoop around the bedroom, studying the old maps on the wall. Nearly every country was pinned with different coloured location markers. *He must have travelled a lot when he was younger.* If she had to play his future bride for the next few days, it was helpful to know details such as a liking for travel.

She shook her head in disbelief. Yesterday they couldn't even be in the same room as each other. Now, she was in his childhood room. She hated that he hadn't told her where he was bringing her, but thinking of his promise gave her some comfort. *Once this is all over, we can go back to ignoring each other and pretend that this never happened, for the sake of the company. This will certainly be a Christmas I'll never forget...*

Several chimes rang throughout the house, and she remembered she was supposed to be at breakfast. Her fifteen minutes of peace were up. She was disappointed not to have time to snoop through the rest of the cabin before everyone woke.

The smell of something delicious wafted down the long hallway. Lyla followed the scent down to the entrance and through the logged archway to a great sitting room with white fluffy beanbags and suede burgundy couches. Above the mantle of another roaring fire was a TV screen, the perfect size for watching old movies on. *An old black and white film, with a cup of hot chocolate.* The thought of chocolate and the smell of what might be pancakes made her mouth water and her stomach gurgle.

The cabin wrapped around in an open plan, and she soon came face to face with Klaus, his brother, and his mother in the kitchen. They looked surprisingly well-put-together so early in the morning, Mrs Klaus in a bright red wrap dress and Kevin in jeans and a hoodie, with a band title on the front Lyla had never heard of. She felt like a slob in Klaus's clothes.

Kevin was setting the table. She wanted to say hi and introduce herself, but Klaus motioned for her to sit without a word. She stared at him, looking like a stranger without his suit. *He's wearing... jeans?* They were black – *like his soul* – but *jeans?*

"So glad you could join us! We thought about letting you sleep on. Travelling by bell can be hard on those not used to it," Mrs Klaus said, appearing behind her and making Lyla jump. "Didn't mean to frighten you," she added teasingly, setting down a tray of various juices.

"There was really no need to go to all this trouble," Lyla said, looking at the table set for a king. She wanted to help, but she got the feeling she would only be in the way; she took a seat.

"What trouble?" Kevin said, looking at the table in confusion.

"Nothing – it's lovely," she said, realising this must be normal for them.

"Don't let Kevin trick you; we don't dine like this every morning," Mrs Klaus said. "We're usually far too busy, but it's not every day we welcome a new member into the family. I wish it could have been done sooner..." She glanced at Klaus, who was currently more interested in the bacon sizzling on the stove than their conversation.

"Nice to meet you, Kevin. Sorry I didn't say hi last night," Lyla said, trying to be polite. The teenager looked at her like she was the mad one.

"No need to be sorry – it's a pleasure to meet me," he said in the same smug tone Klaus often used.

"What has got into you? Don't be so rude to our guest." Mrs Klaus glared at her youngest son. From the look he gave her, he didn't think he had done anything wrong.

"How can I be the only one surprised that Mason has a girlfriend?" Kevin demanded. "No, not even a girlfriend. He got *engaged,* and didn't tell us?"

Lyla suddenly found her plate very interesting. She didn't want to lie to them. *Klaus could have come to wake me... will they think it's strange he hasn't even said good morning? It might have reassured them.* She looked to Klaus, hoping he would save her.

Klaus leaned over her, and for a second she thought he was going to kiss her, but he only picked up a plate of chocolate chip pancakes. "See something you like?" he asked with a grin, and she flushed.

"Plenty," she replied, flustered. "The food looks incredible," she finished, and Klaus's smirk disappeared. He took a seat.

"Can we eat? Or are we going to continue to make Lyla feel uncomfortable?" he said, and took a bite of his pancake. *A sweet tooth? Anyone with a body like his who can eat such stuff should be a crime against nature.*

Mrs Klaus patted Lyla's hand reassuringly on the table, then paused and looked down.

"What a beautiful ring! My great-aunt would have been delighted to know it's being worn by someone, rather than sitting in a jewellery box," she said, and Lyla's answer stuck in her throat. *Did he have to give me a ring with such meaning?*

"I don't know how I didn't notice it last night," Mrs Klaus continued, lifting Lyla's hand. Klaus merely shrugged, leaving it to Lyla to make up an excuse.

"It was resized – it was a little small. Kl— Mason only remembered to give it back to me last night before bed. In the rush to get here, it slipped my mind that I wasn't wearing it," she babbled, hoping no one would notice that her heart was racing.

A female voice came from the hall. "On the life of Saint Nic, it's bloody freezing out there!"

Lyla was grateful for the interruption, and to hopefully meet Klaus's sister.

"Mind your language! We have a guest," Mrs Klaus called as she placed down hot plates of bacon and eggs.

"What?" Klaus whispered. Lyla noticed a crumb of chocolate at the side of his mouth.

"I didn't say anything," she whispered back, not wanting to add to the tension.

"It looks like you want to," he pointed out, and she

found herself staring at his lips. She had never noticed how perfect they were before.

Perfect? He's the devil!

"If another neighbour is dropping off more condolence food, I swear I'll scream. Sara found four stews and a salmon pie on our doorstep this morning before she went to the workshop," she heard the woman say.

Klaus rolled his eyes. "My sister. Sara's her wife," he said to Lyla, getting up.

A woman, clearly the eldest of the three siblings, rolled herself into the kitchen. Lyla hadn't even noticed that the small slope between the living area and the kitchen was designed for a wheelchair.

"You came back! Only took you ten years," Klaus's sister said to him, ignoring everyone else in the room.

"It only took you ten years to ask me to, and when Louise asks, I can hardly say no," Klaus answered, as if she was the general of an army.

Louise didn't look pleased by his tone, but she didn't say anything. The tension made Lyla want to dive under the table.

Luckily, Kevin broke the silence by pushing Klaus towards his sister. All three siblings shared their mother's blonde hair and light blue eyes.

"We're finally together," Kevin pointed out. "Let's not fight." Lyla was surprised by his sudden change in attitude. *Or maybe it's just me he has an attitude for.*

"I hate when you call me that," Louise said. Apparently that was all that needed to be said before Klaus walked over and hugged her.

"Hi, I'm Lyla," Lyla said awkwardly as she made eye contact with Louise, who knocked her brother out of the way with her chair to get a better look at her. Klaus grunted as the footrest hit his shin; Lyla took his pain as her own little victory.

"Lou," Louise said, extending her hand, and Lyla hurried to take it. She had kind eyes, but the same stern look as her brother, which made Lyla uneasy. *I'm going to have to prove myself to her before she trusts me.* "Don't call me Louise, and we'll get along fine," she went on, shaking Lyla's hand.

"Louise who?" Lyla joked, and Lou released her tight grasp on her hand.

"I like her. We might let you keep her," she said to Klaus.

"Are you alright, Lyla? You've gone as white as a sheet!" Mrs Klaus said.

"Fine – just hungry. We shouldn't let all this go to waste," Lyla said with a nervous laugh, wanting everyone's attention off her.

"Don't worry, there's plenty more. The villagers keep bringing us food," Lou told her. Lyla thought of the salmon pie and stews. Her own neighbours had done the same when her mother passed. She'd never wanted to see another shepherd's pie again – although the gifted meals had still been preferable to her father's cooking, or the countless nights of takeaway.

Kevin and Mrs Klaus sat across from Lyla and Mason while Lou took the other end of the table, leaving the head of the table empty. Since everyone was ignoring the empty chair and set place, Lyla did the same.

There was an awkward minute of fork-scraping and glass-clinking before the questions were fired, sadly none of them directed at Klaus.

"How did you meet my loathsome brother?" Lou began, adding a worrying amount of maple syrup to her plate.

"Work. His office is down from mine." Lyla glanced at him as he placed a bowl of chopped fruit salad on the table. She stared nervously at the strawberries in the bowl; hopefully she could avoid them.

"Where's that?" Lou asked as she filled her own plate with the red fruit.

"Smurfit Toys Limited. We make children's toys. We're like the mother company for small businesses. We handle their shipping and PR so they don't have to, as well as having a few of our own brands."

"Toys? You make toys?" Lou smirked. Kevin laughed into his glass of milk; Mrs Klaus tapped his arm and the milk sloshed onto his plate.

"My great-grandfather had his own shop making toys. As the years changed, so did the business. My father ran it, and when he retired..." Lyla paused, not sure how to explain the next part.

"He left it to you?" Mrs Klaus asked eagerly.

"No – he sold his shares of the company to me," Klaus finished flatly in between mouthfuls of bacon and pancakes. "Her father nearly ran it into the ground, so I helped right the ship."

Furious, Lyla jabbed him with her fork under the table. He jumped slightly and glared at her. She rolled her eyes. She'd barely touched him.

"My grandfather left me his shares, so we *share* the company," she explained.

Klaus increased her frustration by adding the fruit salad to her plate. He stared at her in confusion as she stopped eating.

"Aren't you hungry?" He smiled, seemingly trying to make up for his comment about her father. She gripped his leg beneath the table, trying to get him to shut it.

"Is something wrong with the food?" Kevin demanded.

"I can't eat strawberries, remember, honey?" Lyla said through gritted teeth, though she was almost grateful for his attempted poisoning. It interrupted the discussion of how they'd met before she had to jab him again.

"Why not try them? Mum makes a special syrup – you might love them," Klaus offered. She couldn't believe he hadn't worked it out.

"Well, since I didn't see a hospital in the village, I don't think that would be *wise,*" she said tightly.

His face fell as he realised his mistake. Kevin leaned his elbows on the table, staring at them in amusement.

"I'm so sorry, Lyla. Mason didn't say when I was making it. I'll leave them out in future," Mrs Klaus said, taking away the bowl.

"How can you not know strawberries could kill her if you're marrying her?" Kevin interjected, all amusement.

"I simply forgot. It's been a busy few days." Klaus replaced her plate with his own and continued eating as though they hadn't revealed how little they knew about each other.

"Almost killing your fiancée because you forgot her allergies? Not like you to be so forgetful about such a crucial detail," Lou said suspiciously, eyeing the ring on Lyla's finger.

"I'm careful not to have strawberries around, so it's not something that really comes up," Lyla explained, though Lou still looked a little concerned.

"Let's not ruin our breakfast. What were we saying before?" Mrs Klaus said, and Lyla gave her a grateful smile.

"How we met," she reminded her, even if the topic panicked her.

"It must have been hard to give up what you thought would be yours, but the company brought you together.

You were destined to be part of this family! What do you plan on doing with the business now that you're here?" Klaus's mother asked. Everyone stopped eating to stare at Lyla, waiting for her reply.

"We're off until after New Year's, and then it will be back to work," she said, which earned her a few puzzled looks.

"Mason, have you...?" Mrs Klaus started, but he shook his head, stopping her mid-sentence.

"We haven't discussed it yet," was all he said. Lyla dreaded finding out what they had yet to discuss. She wanted to ask him, to force him to explain, but now wasn't the time or place. Anyway, it probably wouldn't matter once they left.

"Plenty of time," Mrs Klaus agreed. "Darling, can you pass me the—?"

She cut off, and Lyla realised she was talking to the empty chair. She didn't need to guess whose seat it had been. She nudged Klaus, but he didn't look up from his plate. The silence dared her to speak, but she held her tongue. She couldn't help the sorrow swelling in her chest as she watched the older woman clear her throat and stand from the table.

"Sorry – I'm not feeling too well. I think I'll go and lie down," Mrs Klaus said softly with a polite nod to Lyla, who returned the gesture, noticing her glassy eyes.

"We have plenty of time to get to know each other. Get some rest," she offered. Klaus gently squeezed her thigh. She didn't know if he was scolding her or thanking her, because he merely continued to eat while his mother left the table.

"She forgets sometimes," Lou told Lyla, placing her fork on her plate. "At least you're both here to stay. It will take the pressure off her, distract her a little."

Lyla's chest tightened. She wanted to help, but it wasn't her place. She was a stranger, and she knew nothing of their lives.

"We're only staying for the season, and then we have to leave," Klaus said.

"You can't be serious. You've only arrived! We'll need you for more than the season," Lou exclaimed. She looked to Kevin. "Can you give us a minute?"

Her younger brother reluctantly got up from the table and left for the sitting room. Lyla wished more than anything to be able to go with him.

"My life is in the city. I'll return for the season every year, but that's the best I can do. There's only a year before Kevin turns eighteen; he can take over once he comes of age," Klaus said, his tone devoid of emotion.

"Those weren't Dad's wishes, and you would have known that if you had been here!" Lou hissed, shoving her plate away.

"I knew exactly what Dad's wishes were, and that's why I left," he snapped.

"I'll give you both some room," Lyla said, getting up, feeling like piggy in the middle.

"Stay," Klaus bit at her, but she dodged his grip and hurried out of the kitchen.

"Always avoiding the conversation. Dad's dead, and you won't face up to your responsibilities. We gave you ten years to explore, and all you've done is make money and a name for yourself," Lou said as Lyla left.

"Have you been keeping tabs on me?" she heard Klaus demand before she was out of earshot. She had a feeling the family's polite welcome wouldn't last long.

Since Kevin was sprawled out on the couch, playing a game on the TV with his headphones on, she couldn't exactly make idle conversation. She walked to the front door and found a pair of Wellington boots. *I'm sure they wouldn't mind.* She was desperate for some air, and she didn't want Lou thinking she was eavesdropping. Slipping the boots on over her thick socks, she grabbed a jacket from the stand and opened the door.

The chill hit her harshly, but once she had followed the snow-covered terrace to the back of the house where a stone-seated area with a fire pit looked out at the mountains behind, she felt peaceful. She sat star-gazing, warming her cold hands at the fire. The sun never rose at this time of year in the North Pole; Klaus might not have told her much about Yule, but she knew that at least. Back home the light pollution never allowed for such a sight, but here, it was though she could reach out and touch every one. The snow had stopped falling, so she could stay out a little longer without worrying about freezing to death.

"If only I could take this view back with me," she murmured.

A snowball struck the back of her head. Ice slipped down the back of her jacket, forcing her to her feet.

"What the fu—" she squealed, shaking her coat so the flecks of snow would fall out.

Klaus stood a few feet away with another snowball in hand.

"You are such a child," she accused, as he marked his aim. "Don't you dare..."

"Never took you for a coward," he said, looking overjoyed by the torment he was inflicting – and had inflicted upon her for the last twelve hours. *I should have left his drunk arse in the office for the whole floor to find.*

"Because I don't want to have a snowball fight?" she asked, hiding behind the stone seat. Thankfully, he dropped the snowball and held his hands up in truce.

"No, because you ran from the table. You're meant to be my buffer. Instead you ran out of the house like it was on fire." Klaus joined her on the other side of the fire.

"I never agreed to be your buffer, or your wife. Or to come to some wonderland that I'm still not sure hasn't been a delusion caused by bad sushi or champagne!" She stared at the porch around the house so she wouldn't have to look up at him as they spoke. She wouldn't give him the satisfaction.

"Keep your voice down! My mum's room is above us," Klaus hissed, pointing to a balcony where the window was lit.

"Fine. I'll be quiet, but can I *please* ask you some questions? And I expect clear answers."

"Shoot – within reason." Klaus's eyes narrowed, daring her to ask.

Now that they were finally alone, she didn't know where to begin. "What is this place?" she asked, looking over her shoulder at the mountains.

"The Moiruilt mountains."

"But where?"

"Technically, the North Pole, but I can't be specific. The mountains create a basin which protects our land and keeps us sheltered from the severe cold. Those beyond the mountain can't find us; it's protected by an ancient magic that I'm not sure anyone living can explain."

That didn't offer her much comfort. "What about planes, or travellers?" She tucked her numb hands in her pockets, not wanting to go back inside until she got her answers, but walking alongside him towards the cabin.

"They would pass through or over the village, thinking nothing is here – it's protected. Always has been. The perimeter is protected too," he added, and there was an edge of warning to his words.

"By what?"

Mason looked to the stars and shrugged. "Some say magic, but if you wish to be more logical you can think of it as an energy force... It depends on your point of view. The wolves also help."

"No one outside of the village knows this place exists?" Lyla reiterated. She'd return to the wolves later.

"Yes and no. People do leave to live in the regular world, but not often. Yule has everything we could need, and those who leave and return often bring back what we don't – again, within reason."

"The village is self-sustaining?" she asked, thinking how wonderful but also isolating such a place could be.

Klaus stopped her as they reached the side of the house. "You don't want to know why I need you to act as my fiancée? Instead, you want to know about how *sustainable* the village is?"

"Are there really wolves?"

"Yes. White wolves, to be specific. They roam the mountains and the woods, but they rarely come close to the village. The lampposts are always lit, and they don't dare to cross them," he said. *That's some relief.* "Wolves and the village? Seems I don't pique your interest in the slightest."

She was well beyond 'piqued', but her safety had seemed like a higher priority than his twisted reasons. "I figured you were less likely to open up about your family, considering..."

"The frosty welcome from my sister and brother? They want me to take over the family business. My dad always wanted me to fill his boots." He said it quickly. Like tearing off a bandage.

"And you didn't want to?" she asked, daring to look at him. He looked disturbingly relaxed without his suit and tie.

"I wanted out. The village is like one giant family, but stifling. When you aren't given the freedom to choose, it can soon feel like a prison," he told her.

"You're the one who trapped me here," she reminded him.

"Trust me, the irony isn't lost on me."

She looked around. Despite being stuck in Yule, she thought this winter wonderland was beautiful. *I haven't seen the village yet; maybe there's more to this place than meets the eye.*

"Why don't you give it a chance this year? Your family obviously want you here."

"I came to visit. To help. That's it." His voice was as stern as though they were back in the office.

"If being a Klaus means what I think it means, though I can't think about that too much or my brain will collapse in on itself, then... you're kind of required this time of year."

She had seen his father's portrait at the end of the hallway. The red suit, the white beard: his heritage was obvious, even if it defied all logic.

"You saw the portrait." Klaus sighed, and she nodded. "You aren't reacting as I thought you would." He frowned, as though waiting for her to combust.

"How am I supposed to react? My insides are screaming, but I don't think my brain has quite processed the insanity of it all," Lyla explained, trying to maintain her calm facade.

"I'll do the job," he said suddenly, and she almost felt... relieved? *Then again, what Christmas lover wants Santa to quit?* "If you stay," he finished.

"I don't understand why you insist on me staying! Your family were perfectly cordial. If you play Santa—"

"You don't *play* at Santa. It's a serious job. I insist on you staying because if I don't have some tie to the outside world, I'll get sucked into the role. Into what they want me to become. If I make the decision to stay, I want it to be my own, and not because of some forced sense of duty."

Lyla understood about duty. She had taken on her family's crumbling business, and she didn't want to lose what her grandfather had built. Unlike Klaus, though, she had never felt forced into it; she wanted to help out of love for her grandfather's memory, and because she genuinely loved being a part of something that brought joy to people.

"I'll maintain our facade, but you have to be nicer to your family. It's clear how much the loss is affecting them; try not to make it worse," she pleaded.

"Make it worse? How am I possibly making it worse? This is how I am," he said defensively, stepping towards her.

"I don't believe that. I saw the smile on your face when you saw your brother, and you even hugged your sister. You aren't a completely heartless tool. Those are not the actions of a man without a heart."

He suddenly found the icicles hanging from the side of the house fascinating, and she considered that she might have been a little too harsh. *Why does he have to bring out the worst in me?*

"Just be a little warmer. Aren't Klauses meant to be warm and jolly?" she teased, earning herself a low chuckle. She walked towards the house, and he followed.

"Why do you care about how my family see me?" Klaus asked, folding his arms over his chest. She didn't like the way he was looking at her – like he was looking through her.

"Because if you make nice and you decide to stay, then I get my company back," she confessed, and he snorted. It was almost a smile, and the warmth in his eyes nearly melted her resolve to loathe him.

"Always working an angle. Naughty or nice, I don't think you would like it if I left. What would make your life interesting if I were to disappear?" His hand grazed hers as they stepped onto the wrap-around porch, and she wondered if it was an accident or intentional.

"There was plenty in my life before you appeared." Even she didn't believe the words as she said them. Her life had been simple, predictable – which was comforting, but not exciting.

"Then who am I to mess with your perfect life? I can't make any promises. You'll have to play the role to perfection."

"Don't worry, I'll be the perfect doting fiancée—"

He suddenly pushed her up against the side of the house. The impact forced a grunt from her, but his hand covered her mouth, preventing her from asking what the hell he was doing. She considered licking it, sure he would be grossed out enough to release her. Then she heard footsteps on the balcony above them, and the echo of faint music. Releasing her slowly, Klaus held a finger to his lips, and looked pointedly towards the balcony. The trees along the perimeter helped protect them from view.

Distracted, she noticed a low hanging branch covered in fresh snow. While he was busy waiting for his mum to head back in, Lyla reached up over his shoulder and pulled the branch down slowly over him. Once the door closed and he glanced down at her, she greeted him with a wink. His confusion only furthering her joy, she let go of the branch. It snapped back, coating him in fresh, powdery snow, doing much more damage than a single snowball.

Stifling her laugh, Lyla slipped out from between him and the house and scurried back inside before he could get his revenge.

CHAPTER EIGHT

Lyla had barely taken off her Wellingtons when Mrs Klaus came down the stairs with a dressing gown over her dress.

"Is everything alright? I heard a shout!"

Lyla shook her head, waiting for Klaus to come through the door. He didn't. "Sorry we disturbed you," she said breathlessly, "we were playing a game."

"Ah to be young and in love," Mrs Klaus teased, rubbing her hands together as the open door let the cold into the house.

Lyla laughed it off. The concept of Klaus and love in the same sentence stirred a discomfort in her she couldn't quite name. She wondered what was keeping him outside.

"Are you feeling better?" she dared to ask. She must have been outside for about an hour, so she hoped Mrs Klaus had got some time to herself.

"Much. Nothing a power nap can't cure. I swear by them. The season has been overwhelming, that's all, and we weren't expecting a new bride. Not that I'm not happy to have you... but it's bittersweet that Henry – Mr Klaus – couldn't meet you himself. He would have been overjoyed to know Mason was happy with someone."

Unable to prevent herself, Lyla wrapped her arms around his mum. She couldn't lie, but she could comfort.

"Sorry," she said, "you looked like you needed a hug. It would have been an honour to meet him." Mrs Klaus squeezed her tight. "With a nap and hug, I think you can take over the world," Lyla added, releasing her.

Mrs Klaus laughed. "What a fine world it would be if everyone thought that way. Would you care for a hot chocolate? Or I have some coffee? My nerves are a little unsettled for the stuff – Henry was always the coffee drinker. I'm sure you'd love a cup, since Ireland is nine hours ahead of us."

Nine hours ahead? It would already be afternoon back home. *Hopefully it won't take too long for me to adjust.*

"I'd love a hot chocolate too. I understand being overwhelmed – this trip certainly has been a lot, and I don't think caffeine will help," Lyla said, and took a seat on the couch.

The soft cushions cradled her body like a duvet, and she could have fallen asleep then and there in front of the roaring fireplace. But it wasn't long before Mrs Klaus returned with two mugs. She handed Lyla a mug with a gingerbread man on the front and a candy cane handle.

"Would you like a little brandy in it? Warms the soul," she said, taking a bottle out from behind a book on the shelf. Lyla remembered that Klaus had the same brand in his apartment.

I can't believe I'm having hot chocolate with Mrs Klaus.

"No, I'm fine, thank you. I think I have a hard time believing this is all really happening without getting drink involved," Lyla joked, not pointing out that it was the early morning. "I mean, the trip was so impromptu, and K— Mason hasn't said much about where he's from, or about his family. I didn't even know he had a sister until the letter arrived." She scolded herself internally for tripping up over his name again. *From now on, he is Mason!*

"I doubt he's been very open. He's the secretive one in the family – you'd never know what he's thinking, but he has a good heart. There's only so much he could reveal, given that our family is more legend in your world than fact. If he had told you without bringing you, I'm sure you'd have thought he belonged in a padded room," Mrs Klaus said, putting the bottle back after adding a generous measure to her mug.

"You're probably right. I know his last name is Klaus, but he's such a Scrooge in the office – I never would have guessed the truth." The warmth of the mug was finally returning the feeling to Lyla's hands.

"It's a big responsibility to be born with. Henry and he argued a lot, and when he decided to leave, it was heartbreaking. Not just for us, but it worried many of our workers, as it made their future uncertain."

"Still, being kept in the dark is not all that fun," Lyla said, taking a sip of the richest hot chocolate she'd ever tasted. "This is so good I think I'm ruined for life."

"I do wish he had told you something. Once you were engaged, he could have told you, but our laws are strict about outsiders. I was an outsider myself, and it was quite a shock, but I had the choice. Mason should have done the same for you before bringing you into the family." She didn't sound angry, but there was hurt in her voice.

"He probably thought because I come from such a small family – it's only me and my dad – that I would be happy to discover a big family was here." Lyla wasn't entirely sure why she was defending him, but she didn't want any more strain on his relationship with his mother, and she certainly didn't want to be the cause of it.

"Lord knows what goes through that man's head. I didn't know when he was a young lad, and I still don't!"

Lyla saw an opportunity. "Is there any way I can send a message home to my dad? I didn't bring my phone or laptop, and I didn't get a chance to tell him I was leaving," she said, though she was pretty sure her father wouldn't notice, since he was on his honeymoon.

"Absolutely. I wouldn't want him to think anything has happened to you. There's a laptop in my office – third door on the left in the south wing. Just follow the glass corridor out the kitchen. Can't go wrong."

"Thank you! I promise I won't be long with it when I get the chance," Lyla said. She didn't plan on moving yet; she was enjoying Mrs Klaus's company.

"You're family now, borrow it whenever you need. We have rather limited technology here. The mountains protect us from the outside, and we try to keep communication to a limit. But many of us have kids in the outside world, so we can't be completely cut off." Mrs Klaus seemed to relax as she drank. It was nice to see her features brighten.

"It's like something out of a fairytale – a protected village," Lyla said, trying not to sound too awed.

"I suppose I've got used to it. Travelling by sleigh, the eternal winter, magic bells... it can be very overwhelming at first, especially when you join the Klaus family with its own traditions and responsibilities to the village. I was once like you, so I understand how you must be feeling."

Mrs Klaus's words only added to the many questions Lyla had. *Then again, do I really need the answers if I'm leaving?* But she wanted to hear this story.

"Like me?" she dared to press.

"Henry and I met in the outside world. I was working in a bakery when he came in. He ate more cookies than a man with such an exquisite physique should be able to in one sitting, and for three days in a row he came back. On the third day, he left a note asking for a date. When he came back on the fourth day, I said yes. The following Christmas, I was pregnant with Lou and haven't regretted a day since. Adjusting to life here is hard, but I think the rewards outweigh the losses." Mrs Klaus blushed as she recounted the story, but thinking of good memories seemed to make the hard day easier for her.

"But you grew up out there. Didn't your friends and family miss you?" Lyla wondered.

"They did, at first, but friends grow up and apart. I told them I'd moved to another country. We wrote letters. It was much harder to keep track of each other then, and soon letters stopped as the distance and time passed. I found new friends here. There are many outsiders who marry and come here, so you don't feel so alone, and then we all slot together like one big jigsaw puzzle. Yule has its own magic – everyone who visits falls in love with it."

"I understand the pull. I've been obsessed with Christmas since my mum first hung the star on the tree. Yule is a Christmas village dream come true, but it's such a sacrifice," Lyla mused. She couldn't imagine leaving her friends, her mother's townhouse – except maybe she could for a family she loved, for the person she loved.

"Mason leaving made me realise what my family must have felt... maybe what they still feel. I still send Christmas letters to my brother, but that's it. There is a price for love, but I would happily pay it again if it meant spending another day with Henry. Plus, now that Mason has found someone, I think it was worth missing him. He bought me the laptop to email him, but we prefer to keep to letters, and it was hard to keep in touch," Mrs Klaus said, changing the subject. Lyla could count on one hand the number of times she had written an actual letter. "I suppose you saw the letter Lou wrote. I asked her not to, but being the eldest and overseeing the workshop, there was no stopping her. Kevin has to wait until he is eighteen to fulfil the role, should it remain empty. For now, he helps with the reindeer and other small tasks."

"Mason might seem like he doesn't want to be here, but I can see how much he loves you all. Just coming here has softened him. I'm happy to lend him as an extra set of hands, but can I ask what exactly you need him for?"

Mrs Klaus laughed.

"There can't be a Christmas without him. Come rain or hail, sun or storm, Christmas must take place," she said seriously.

Lyla tried not to stare disbelievingly. She knew the truth, and yet it seemed so ridiculous. *Mason as Santa?* The irony was overwhelming. It was strange enough to think of him as Mason instead of the budget-slashing Mr Klaus.

"I know it's hard to believe, but we are the generations of Klaus. Our ancestors were tasked with spreading joy through the world. I know it doesn't make much sense to you now, and it's a lot for you to take in. If you could have a little faith and patience, I'm sure Mason will explain everything. He never expected this burden to fall on him; he wanted more than our small village. He wanted to see the world, but after Lou had her accident, Mason was next in line. Don't get me wrong, she can still do the job, but she prefers to work in sleigh engineering."

When Mrs Klaus didn't elaborate on the accident, Lyla didn't pry. She'd never considered that Mason wasn't only returning to mourn his father, but also to face a future he didn't want and had little choice in. "I can't exactly picture Mason climbing down a chimney. His designer suits wouldn't stand the test," she laughed, knowing how uptight he was about his clothes.

"Actually, not all the myths are true. We don't give gifts. We give something else much less tricky," Mrs Klaus was saying, when Mason came in. He appeared fully recovered from Lyla's snow bomb, which disappointed her.

"Mum, I think we've bombarded Lyla with enough information for one day," he said. Mrs Klaus pretended to zip her lips closed. "We should get to the village, because I don't think she wants to wear my clothes for the rest of the season."

He placed a hand on Lyla's shoulder, and she put the mug on the table and rose to join him, eager to get out of his clothes.

Mrs Klaus sighed, putting down her own mug. "I suppose you're right, and I have a luncheon to attend for the charity auction. See you in the evening – and Mason, don't forget there's the gala in a few days. You'll need to find her a dress to wear," Mrs Klaus said, stopping them in their tracks as they made for the door.

"I don't think we're going to attend this year. Lyla has only arrived, and this is such a busy time of year. Everyone is stressed – not the best time to introduce her..." Mason began.

Mrs Klaus raised her eyebrows in warning. "Don't be silly; everyone is home for the season. It's the perfect time to introduce her."

Lyla wanted to argue, but didn't know what to say without revealing their secret. The last thing she wanted was to be introduced to the whole village when she was a fraud. *Mason, what the hell have you got us into?*

"Fine. Since Lyla isn't opposed, we shall attend," Mason said. Lyla wanted to protest, but it was too late now.

"Glad to see you've started listening to someone else," Mrs Klaus said. She winked at Lyla, who could only force a half-smile as Mason led her out the door.

CHAPTER NINE

It took Lyla some time to adjust to the villagers staring at them as they made their way through the village. The streets were packed, so they blended in nicely. Though it was slightly suffocating, being outside made it more bearable. The only break she got was popping into shops, where Lyla was enraptured with the antiques, homemade crafts such as quilts and ceramics. Bakeries filled the air with the most delicious scent. She wanted to go inside every one, the pastries in the window calling to her, but Klaus pulled her along, stating there was too much to be done.

Thankfully, there were also more everyday shops, like clothes stores and grocery shops. Lyla felt pity for Mason, who was occasionally accosted by proprietors or shoppers about his visit. Luckily for her, most were too busy running around gathering their supplies for Christmas or working too hard to care too much about her. She was smart enough to scurry away before she could be introduced and Mason did an excellent job at avoiding their questions, but he was still polite, and she was surprised he took their prying on the chin. If anyone in the office had dared question him like this, they would have been tossed out of the room by the mere power of his glare.

She was soon sweaty in her many layers and tired, but she found everything she needed for daily use: jeans, knitted jumpers, thermal tops and a pair of much-needed boots. She'd also managed to get the right products for her hair, and a diffuser. She also treated herself to some nice underwear, since her outerwear was more functional than fashionable. In *that* shop, she forced Mason to wait outside. The shop assistant put it on Mrs Klaus' account; Lyla would pay it back once they were home.

"How about some food? We've been at this for hours," she groaned in the dress shop, glancing at the clock. They had already been here for an hour and hadn't found anything for the gala.

"This is the last stop, and then you can eat as much as you like," Mason said, which was all the encouragement she needed to try on yet another dress – an orange tulle dress with a full skirt suggested by the assistant.

"Are you almost ready?" Mason called from outside the dressing room.

Lyla wished Mrs Klaus had taken her; Mason had zero patience. She couldn't believe she was actually dress shopping with him. She gauged her appearance in the mirror, looking and feeling like a cheap tangerine Cinderella.

"I think this is the worst yet," she chuckled, opening the curtain, and Mason stifled a laugh by rubbing his jaw. The assistant beside him looked deeply offended and left with a quick tut.

"I've seen you wear worse," Mason said once he was gone.

"*When* have you seen me wear worse? I could stop traffic!" Lyla fluffed up the skirt. He laughed, and for a moment she thought maybe they could be friends.

She stopped messing around when a woman approached, afraid that the shop owner was coming to kick them out for insulting her dresses. She was about to apologise when the woman, who had gorgeous blonde waves, sneered at her and turned to Mason.

"Mace? I would recognise that laugh anywhere!" The woman beamed, sauntering over to him.

Lyla felt like a gooseberry standing in the changing room as the woman kissed his cheek. The sensation the sight caused disturbed her more than the bright yellow dress the woman – roughly the same age as Mason – was wearing.

"Natalie. I didn't think we'd run into you here," Mason said, looking a little troubled. Lyla relaxed slightly at being included, but Natalie ignored her.

"You should come to the pub tonight; we're all back for the season. We've missed you over the years! It's a pity your father couldn't see us reunited," Natalie said, and Lyla knew that what the woman truly meant was that *she* missed him.

"I don't think tonight is a good idea. We have a lot to do – we've only just arrived." Mason was being polite, but Lyla could see the discomfort in his eyes. It was the same look he gave her when he wanted a client meeting to end sooner rather than later.

"Is this your friend? There has been talk of a new outsider in the village," Natalie said, looking Lyla up and down as if she was an animal in the zoo. The upturned corner of her mouth reeked of disgust. Before Lyla could stop herself, she was wrapping herself under Mason's arm and placing a possessive hand on his abdomen.

"Hi, I'm Lyla," she said, offering Natalie her hand. "His fiancée."

"Lyla, this is Natalie," Mason said, when the woman only stared at the ring on Lyla's extended hand.

"What a beautiful ring. His f-fiancée?" Natalie stuttered, her cheeks brightening to a red that threatened to overtake the red wallpaper of the shop. "I hadn't heard. I should congratulate you both." But she didn't – she merely offered Mason a pinched smile and left.

Mason cleared his throat, and Lyla poked him.

"I never thought jealousy would look so good on you," he mused.

She rolled her eyes at him in the mirror. "Jealous? She was looking at me like I was the ugly duckling while you were the swan." Mortified by being seen in such a dress, she tried to reach the zip on the back. "Who was she?" she added, dying to know what he was hiding.

"Ex-girlfriend. She fancied herself the next Mrs Klaus. Then I left, but she and my father never let go of the idea." Mason offered the information like it was nothing, but from the look in Natalie's eyes, she thought Lyla was treading on her territory.

"I thought Mrs Klauses were outsiders?" she said, stepping back inside the changing room and trying the zip again. It seemed to be stuck.

"You've been talking with my mother. Not always, but most." Klaus stepped up behind her and brushed her hand away. "Need some help?"

He didn't wait for a response before his fingertips gripped the zip and traced it down her spine until he reached the edge of her underwear. Lyla's skin prickled, and her breath caught. Her eyes found his in the mirror, and she saw something in them – something she hadn't seen before. Before she could ponder what she felt between them, she closed the curtain on him, afraid she might not like the answer. Her hands on her hips, she thought of his hands on her and shook away the thought of them dipping lower.

"Do you need my help again?" Mason said mockingly from the other side of the curtain.

"Give me a minute," she called, pulling on the last dress of the pile: a rich, red satin gown. The way the satin flowed over her curves was enough to make her want to wear it every day. Luckily, there was some boning and cups in the bust so a bra wouldn't ruin the low back.

"Dying of old age," Mason called. When Lyla opened the curtain, he was sitting with his elbows on his knees, staring at the wooden floorboards.

"How about this one?" she asked, drawing his eyes to her.

When she saw him swallow, she knew it was a winner. His mouth fell open while his eyes traced every inch of her body, lingering on her exposed shoulders until they finally settled on her face.

"Something to say?" she asked, turning to face the mirror, exposing the low back where the fabric draped at her waist.

"It's perfect," he said, rising to stand behind her again, his voice low. "But something isn't right."

Lyla groaned, wondering what else it could possibly need.

"Get changed. I'll have a word with the assistant," Mason said, suddenly disappearing to the front of the store.

Lyla was nonplussed. *Does he want the dress or not?* He hadn't said to bring it to the counter, so she left it on the hook. When she joined him, a deal seemed to have been struck; Mason was placing a few gold coins, the same she had seen him use all morning, into the assistant's hand. *Is he ordering the dress? Why is he being so secretive about a damn dress?*

"Your order will take some time, but we'll have it delivered to your house on the day of the gala," the assistant assured them, though Lyla wasn't sure what would be arriving.

"I don't think I could ever get used to this," she said once they were out on the street. Despite the cold, she was glad to be out of the stuffy dressing room. "Where do you even get those coins? I didn't ask earlier because I was having too much fun spending them. Now that we're finished, I want to know." She kept close so people on the street wouldn't hear her.

"The gold comes from the mountains. Since we're cut off from the rest of the world, we have our own currency."

That surprised her, but why shouldn't they? Many countries had their own currency.

"So how do you trade with the outside world?" she asked, wondering how they went about sourcing outside goods.

"We aren't completely cut off. We have a bank to exchange the gold for other currencies when we need to trade. Many of our people who've left over the years to work in the outside world are able to source what we need without leaving a trace." Klaus walked ahead of her at an exaggeratedly leisurely pace.

"Sounds awfully complicated."

"Complicated? What place isn't?"

"Surely if someone is trading with Yule, they'll have questions about where the goods were being sent?" she pressed, but he merely shrugged.

"You'd be amazed how little people care about where the goods are going, as long as they get paid, and get paid well."

Lyla was beginning to understand how he knew the business world so well for someone so young. "All the secrets, making sure nobody finds out the truth... it must take up a lot of time," she said, wondering how they had managed to keep Yule secret for so long. *Bribery? False documents?* She wasn't sure she wanted to know, and she doubted he was going to tell her everything about his home.

"In Yule," he told her, "there's only one season to rush. Otherwise, it's the most tranquil place in the world."

CHAPTER TEN

The following morning, Lyla woke before the rest of the house and found her way to the office Mrs Klaus had mentioned. Icicles had formed along the outer glass wall, making her feel like she was walking through an ice palace. Knocking softly on the door, she made sure no one was inside.

"Wow!" she exclaimed at the chaos within. Shelves full of scrolls and old leather-bound books lined the walls, broken only by an imposing family portrait hung above a great mantle covered in holly. The family in the painting seemed to date back a few generations. *Probably a couple of centuries, judging from the style.* Lyla's mum being an artist gave her some insight into art, but she couldn't tell exactly when it was from. Two wooden desks sat across from each other on either side of the room – it was cosy, in spite of the chaos.

The fire was out. She considered leaving it, but it was far too cold. All it took was a spark to get it going.

No more distractions. Find the laptop! She wasn't sure whose desk was whose until she noticed the half-open laptop on the one closest to the door. At Mrs Klaus's desk, Lyla pushed aside the letters and what looked to be beautifully addressed invitations – *must be for the gala* – and opened the laptop, breathing a sigh of relief when there was no need for a password.

The internet was incredibly slow, and watching it connect only irritated her further. While she waited, Lyla gathered up some of the books from the floor and placed them on the shelves. When curiosity got the better of her, she pulled out one of the scrolls from a shelf marked with a brass 1990s plaque. Once it was unfurled, she gasped. In her hand was the 'Naughty and Nice list 1991'. Scanning the seemingly never-ending list, she figured she would never find her own name, but when she ran her fingers over the gold letters, it suddenly lit up on the 'Nice' column. She smiled at the comfort of it.

Would a Klaus be on the list? she wondered, thinking of Mason. *How was the list even written?*

The laptop chimed, breaking her train of thought, and she placed the scroll back on the shelf. Reclaiming her seat, she found herself staring at the lonely desk across the way and understood how hard it must be for Mrs Klaus to see the chair remain empty each day since his passing. *If Mason stayed, he could take the desk and she wouldn't have to work alone.*

If he did decide to stay, it also meant she would get control of her company again. Without him, she could run it the way she'd always wanted, without any interference.

Finally connected to the internet, she sent an email

to Sam. He would be eager to hear her plans, even if she couldn't disclose everything, or even understand everything herself.

> Sam,
>
> I don't have much time, but I hope you're having a nice break. I'm sorry to let you know like this, but I must cancel our plans for Christmas dinner. Please apologise to Jamie for me! I was looking forward to it. Something has come up that I can't really explain. Don't ask because I can't tell you where I am, but I had to take a trip to a rather extraordinary place. Don't worry about me either; I'll be home after the holidays. I need you to do me a favour – it's of the utmost importance. In my office, there are the documents for transferring company shares. Everything has already been drafted. I need you to scan them and send me the files. I'll explain everything when I return.
>
> Please respond to this address and not my own. I didn't take my phone or laptop with me. I'll delete this email afterwards, so please return the requested documents with a different title and subject. I don't want to have to explain in case my plans turn out differently. But if everything goes the way I hope, we might have a new CEO soon and one less financial advisor.
>
> Give my best to Jamie, and I'll see you in the New Year!
> Lyla x

She deleted the sent email and made sure to remove it from Mrs Klaus' trash. Guilt seeded in her gut as soon as the SENT notification appeared, but if everything worked out... *It'll be a win–win for all. There'll be a new Mr Klaus, and I'll get my company.*

The guilt wouldn't go away as she closed the door behind her. *His father just died, and I'm scheming to get my company back!* She silenced her inner voice by reminding herself that he never should have been involved in her company in the first place. He was the one who had kidnapped her and brought her here without telling her there might be the chance of her getting her memory wiped. His family needed him here; the company was only holding him back. The world shouldn't be deprived of a Santa Claus. She had to make him see that, and she only had a few days to convince him. *If he decides not to stay, then he'll be none the wiser,* she assured herself.

She decided a walk would be the best way to quiet her mind and soothe her conscience. Desperate for some air, she put on her new long black coat over her wide-leg jeans and white jumper. She was glad she'd listened to Mason and gone up half a size in the boots, because they fitted perfectly over her fluffy socks. Heading outside, Lyla walked the property until she came to the stables. Finding a bucket of carrots, she got as close as she dared to the reindeer in their individual pens. The first she came to read 'Vixen' on the collar. She sniffed the air as Lyla moved closer.

"Hey, girl, fancy a carrot?" The animal stared between Lyla and the bucket with big brown eyes. Her reaching out was enough to startle the reindeer, who backed away. "It's okay! I didn't mean to frighten you," Lyla said, stopping her approach.

"Be careful," said Mason from the doorway. "Vixen likes to bite. She gets excited when she sees carrots, and suddenly she can't tell the difference between fingers and vegetables."

"We were getting along fine," Lyla lied, backing away from Vixen. Mason scoffed and took a carrot from the bucket.

"Here, hold it like this," he said, placing it in her hand and standing behind her so she couldn't recoil from the creature. "She won't bite you if you're confident." He nudged her forward.

The reindeer stepped closer, sniffing Lyla's open hand and the treat within. Lyla winced and found herself buried in Mason's chest, but he held firm, wrapping her fingers around the carrot.

"I never pegged you for being afraid of such a harmless reindeer."

His breath at her ear made her aware of how dangerously close they were. The chomp of the carrot distracted her and she dropped it and stumbled back, kicking over the bucket as she escaped his embrace.

"What? *I'm* not the one who was going to bite," Mason said, picking up the bucket. Vixen was eating the fallen carrot without a care for them.

"I'm not so sure," Lyla said under her breath, composing herself.

"Since you're done frightening the reindeer – I've been looking for you. You weren't in your room," he said, offering Dancer a carrot while Lyla followed him.

"I couldn't sleep. Thought a walk would help," she lied.

"It's good you're already dressed. I've had a messenger deliver a note," Mason said, and she noticed that he was paler than usual. She sensed what he was about to say was nothing good, but she let him finish. "The council has got word of your arrival, and they would like to meet you."

"I was wondering what had you looking so white. It's not like you're the one facing the guillotine," Lyla pointed out.

Donner stuck out her nose, shoving Lyla towards Mason. She glared at the animal, who only went back to eating her straw.

"Don't be ridiculous. They wouldn't use a guillotine." He winked, and she wondered how many more times today she'd want to slap away his arrogance.

"When do they want to meet?" She tried not to sound nervous, but she doubted she was successful.

"They've called a morning meeting. It shouldn't take too long." She didn't know if he was trying to reassure her or himself.

"Could someone have found out you... *we* lied?" She looked back to the house and couldn't help but doubt them. *They seem friendly, but would they sacrifice me for the safety of their village?*

"You're overthinking this. They merely wish to meet you; they're required to meet every outsider. Tell them what we've told my family. We work together in the outside world. We got engaged, and then decided to quickly return due to my father's passing and had no time to inform anyone." Mason rattled off the lies like her memory wasn't hanging in the balance.

"Easy for you to say. You aren't the outsider."

"I wouldn't be too sure. My decision to leave wasn't popular. There are many who are happy about my return, but some would rather I hadn't."

"Is that supposed to reassure me of my safety?" *Who didn't want him back?*

"No, but I can assure you that we'll both feel equally uncomfortable."

They left the stables, where the reindeer didn't seem half as scary now compared to what Lyla was about to face. Argyle pulled into the driveway, waving them over, and there was no chance for further discussion.

CHAPTER ELEVEN

They had passed the town hall while shopping the previous day. It was a church-like structure, as intimidating as its architecture was unique.

Mason kept slightly behind her the whole time, and she figured he was afraid she was going to turn and run. She would be lying if she said the thought hadn't crossed her mind.

Walking through the doors into a room that looked like it belonged in a gothic tale, they approached the reception desk in the corner and were greeted by a stoic individual with a clipboard and an upturned nose.

"This way. The council have been waiting," the receptionist said, leading them through the corridor to a grand ballroom, at the far end of which sat a panel of all ages talking amongst themselves. They were all dressed in suits or fine clothes, and Lyla felt significantly underdressed in her jeans and winter coat. The last thing she needed was for them to judge her on appearance before she had a chance to introduce herself.

Mason gave her hand a squeeze before dropping it. "You look fine. Don't fidget," he whispered. He was standing far too close, and she almost leaned away before remembering they were supposed to be engaged. When they reached the panel, she took his hand again and gripped it tightly, not allowing him to let go.

"We have been waiting," a stout man older than the rest said.

"I only received your message this morning. You hardly gave us a moment to get ourselves together," Mason said defensively. "I'm sure you won't hold it against us, Uncle Fred."

The use of the nickname turned the man purple.

"That would be Councilman Frederick," he said sternly. "I'm not your uncle in this room."

Lyla noticed an empty seat along the table. She wondered if Mrs Klaus was meant to be here. *Maybe she wasn't invited because this meeting involves her own family.*

"I didn't realise this was to be such a formal introduction," Mason said.

Another council member in a beige suit spoke up. "We haven't seen or heard from you in ten years. Now you come back and want to pretend that everything is as it was, along with expecting us to accept a fiancée we've never met? Surely you can understand our hesitation."

Mason gripped her hand painfully tight.

"Una, I meant no insult to you, the council, or Yule in my leaving or return. I merely wish to aid my family this season and to be a part of my father's send-off," he said.

The council murmured amongst themselves.

"And we are to simply accept your return after such a period?" Frederick said.

Lyla opened her mouth to defend Mason but silenced herself. It would probably only hurt him more if an outsider spoke up for him.

"Many leave for more than ten years before returning. Just because I'm a Klaus, it seems I'm being penalised for it. If anything, my experience in the world will benefit Yule. Though I'm sure you would have preferred me not to return at all, uncle," he said coldly.

Lyla remembered Mrs Klaus mentioning that Kevin was too young to take over the position. Perhaps the uncle had thought he'd inherit the position if Mason didn't return. Even so, she didn't know if now was the right time to be so direct – not when they needed the council's trust.

"Of course we are pleased to see you return, but some warning would have been appreciated." Frederick huffed, clearly not appreciating having his intentions called out.

"We are being rude to our guest," Una put in, looking from Frederick to Lyla with a faint smile. Lyla would have preferred the uncle's attention remained off her, but it was too late.

"Tell us about yourself. If you are to be the future Mrs Klaus, we need to know more about you. Mason should have brought you to us the day you arrived – he knows the rules," Frederick said, though he didn't seem very interested in what she had to say.

"I would have, but I figured you would all have much more important things to do, given the season is only around the corner," Mason began, and Lyla squeezed his hand in warning.

Before he could continue, she hastily said, "My name is Lyla Smurfit, and I hope you don't mind me saying, but Mason had no intention of surprising you with our arrival. Our engagement was rather fast, and when we became aware of his father's passing, we decided to return. We had hoped to return and make the announcement at a better time, but I couldn't let him return alone after losing his father."

"It's well and good to make excuses, but you are an outsider. What is your background?" Frederick demanded.

"I run a company which specialises in toys. I'm an only child. My father has resigned from our company, which Mason and I manage together," Lyla said, throwing together the first facts that came to mind.

"What would you tell your family, your friends, if you were to reside here? Our secrecy is what keeps our legacy alive," said another council member with startlingly thick brows.

"My mother passed away when I was in school. My father recently remarried. I have few friends within the company. There aren't too many people to worry about telling," she confessed, trying not to make herself sound like a total loner. "I have a cat, Jones – but he came with me." This addition got a few chuckles, and she was glad for the break in tension.

"You met while working together?" Una enquired.

"We did," Mason said. Lyla had to stop herself from sighing in relief at the pause in the barrage of questions. "It wasn't love at first sight – we could barely tolerate each other – but over time, her passion for the business, her heart for her clients and compassion for those who work under her made me fall in love with her."

Lyla forgot about the council and stared at him. His words sounded so believable that they threatened to stop her heart.

"There's a fine line between love and hate," someone commented, but she wasn't sure who because she was still staring at Mason.

"You can say that again," Lyla replied, chuckling. Mason gripped her hand and she silenced herself, not wanting to reveal how surprised and confused she was by his words.

"We realise our questioning might seem extreme, but we are incredibly protective of our little community. If anyone chooses to betray its existence to the outside world or threaten us in any way, we take it very seriously. We give all outsiders who plan to join us one chance to leave. We will wipe your memory with a tonic, and you can return to your life without the weight of our secret," Frederick offered.

The offer made her wonder if someone was pouring doubts about their relationship into the council's ears, but Lyla considered it for a split second. Although the idea had terrified her since Mason had mentioned it, she realised that it might actually solve her problems. *I'd no longer be stuck in this strange place, and I wouldn't have Mason interfering with my personal life.* However, if her memory was wiped then she wouldn't know what the consequences for Mason would be. Would she remember him at all? *He may not be my favourite person in the world, but he's shown me magic exists... and brought me closer to the season my mother loved. I don't want to lose that.*

"Excuse me, but Lyla's the last person who would betray Yule. She loves the season and the meaning behind it more than any other rational human being I've known. She'll stay in Yule for as long as she'll have me," Mason said.

"No need for that tone. I've known you since you were a baby, but to return after years and with an outsider – you can understand why the council must be on alert," Frederick argued.

"I understand, but the season is ours to manage. Lyla is merely our guest, and as a Klaus you should treat her with respect!" Mason snapped.

The council went silent.

"Lyla, thank you for putting up with us today." Una was the first to speak, and Lyla was grateful for the understanding. "I'm sure you can understand our trepidation. We are without a Klaus so close to Christmas; tensions are running a little high."

"Speaking of Klaus, when are we to expect an answer from you? The position has to be filled, and not just for this year," Frederick said, clearly eager for an immediate answer.

Mason visibly stiffened. "Soon."

"By the Gala you must make the announcement, as tradition dictates," Frederick ordered. Mason nodded in acknowledgment, and they were waved from the room.

"Why do I feel like we were chastised by the headmaster?" Mason said once they exited the town hall. Thankfully, the steps outside the hall were empty, so they could talk freely.

"Your uncle is a real peach. Felt like they were going to bring out a guillotine at any moment," Lyla said, relieved to escape with her neck and head still attached.

"They're angry at me, not you. They want an answer that I'm not ready to give, and you're an easy target. Frederick and my mum have been sharing this season's duties, and I'm not sure he wants to give up his temporary position."

"If he finds out we're lying, won't he take the choice from you?"

"It would be up to the council to decide. He's only one member," Mason said.

"Is this your plan? To be discovered and thrown out? You can't make the decision, so you want them to make it for you?" She didn't want to be used as a pawn in anyone's game.

He stared at her and scoffed. "Is that how little you think of me? That I would use you to ruin my chances of taking my father's position? I knew your opinion of me was low, but I've always done what was necessary. I've made the hard choices. Leaving here was one of them, but it was the right decision, just as returning was the right thing to do," he said, raking his hands through his hair. Frustration emanated from him in waves.

"It's not that I think little of you. It's that I don't think you understand how your decisions are affecting me. You left of your own free will, and yes, you returned for the right reasons, but you brought me with you!" She didn't want to have this fight in front of the hall, but her emotions were getting the better of her.

"I told you I couldn't come back alone. I wanted you here, but not to use you." His pained expression told her he wanted to say more, but he didn't.

"But how can we keep lying like this? And to those who care about you so much? You've broken their trust and made me the face of such a deception. You might be cast out, but I'll be the one physically altered," she said, exasperated by the cold and the fragility of their situation. It was one thing to take a memory tonic by choice, but quite another to be forced to have it against her will.

"Please. We can't do this here," he pleaded.

Lyla made to reply but was silenced as Mason pulled her flush against him, his hand gripping the back of her neck. Then his lips were on hers, and she was too surprised to think.

He didn't move; the light touch of his lips begged for her consent. She thought about pushing him away, but found her lower lip brushing his, inviting him in. His lips were all warmth and welcome – everything he wasn't. He deepened the kiss, and the sensation made her stomach swoop. His hands gripped her waist beneath her coat, his strength causing her to gasp. She had never known a kiss to feel so right and wrong before.

Suddenly, Mason pulled away and Lyla was snapped back to the cold light of day. She stared at him in confusion, but he only sighed, his gaze fixed over her shoulder. She tried to compose herself. Nothing as simple as a kiss should have possibly felt so exhilarating.

"Sorry. I should have asked you first, but my uncle and the council were coming out and I couldn't have them see us arguing," he explained, sounding breathless at the thought of being caught mid-argument.

Lyla's humiliation swelled as she realised she had kissed him back, and fury filled her when she caught him watching her, trying to gauge her reaction. The worst part was that she had enjoyed the kiss.

You don't want to kiss him; he surprised you, and you're human. Who doesn't like being kissed? Even if it is by a Scrooge who brought you here against your will, and it was only to shut you up. She stared at Mason as he acknowledged the passing council. *Did he want to kiss me? Was it an excuse?*

When his attention returned to her, she couldn't find the words to speak. Rather than say something she'd regret, she forced herself to smile sweetly in case anyone was watching. A fight in the town square was exactly what the council would need to doubt them.

On the way home she opted for the silent treatment, hoping some distance between them would remind her that Mason Klaus was the *last* person she should want to kiss.

CHAPTER TWELVE

For the remainder of the day, Lyla kept to the house while Mason went to the workshop. After a nap and a long shower, she felt more like herself. When Mrs Klaus called her for dinner she considered pretending to be asleep, but her rumbling stomach quickly voided that option.

Mason tried to talk to her as she helped set the table, but she simply nodded along. Looking at him only made her think of the kiss. He gave up once everything was ready, and she took the opportunity to sit across from him instead of at his side.

She needed to get her feelings in check, and pretending to be a couple was too confusing. *How could one kiss throw me so off balance?* Lost in her own thoughts, she barely noticed that the family ate their dinner in silence until dessert – a rhubarb crumble that Lyla, along with the rest of the table, couldn't resist.

"I didn't think you would be able to get away from the workshop. It's a pity Sara couldn't join us," Mrs Klaus said to Lou, who was feeding Jones scraps beneath the table. They had let him out of Lyla's room to roam.

"I know. One of the sleigh engines isn't working, and she won't leave until she figures out why. I'll bring her some food in a bit and then try get her home at a reasonable hour," Lou said, sounding utterly exhausted.

"You should have replaced the parts like I suggested," Kevin said, rolling his eyes.

"We were expecting more parts, but with Dad gone, the order wasn't put through in time." Lou's voice was quiet, as though she didn't want to blame her father.

All eyes fell to Mason. He didn't even look up from his food. Lyla would have given all the gold coins in Yule to know what he was thinking.

"I'm sure she can figure it out," Mrs Klaus said, though the tension could have been cut with a knife. She turned to Lyla. "How did your meeting go with the council?"

Lyla choked on her crumble. She covered her mouth, and Kevin, beside her, patted her back.

"That well?" he joked, and Lyla nodded in thanks as he handed her some water. She took a sip and looked to Mason, hoping he would answer his mother.

"Frederick gave us a grilling. I think he's rather cosy in Dad's seat," he said, putting down his fork.

"Your dad wouldn't want you saying such things about his brother. He's grieving, and worried about the season," Mrs Klaus rebuked him.

"Worried about Mason taking his position, more like," Kevin said.

Lou threw the piece of ham she was going to give to Jones at him. Lyla was surprised that the cat didn't lunge after it, but he seemed far too cosy on Lou's lap.

Kevin dodged it and grimaced at his sister. "What? It's the truth! I bet he thought with Mason gone, he was guaranteed the seat. Out of the blue, big bro comes back and with a new Mrs Klaus." He looked at his mother. "No offence, but Uncle Fred was hardly going to roll out the welcome mat."

"I didn't come back for the seat. I came back to say goodbye to Dad," Mason said sombrely.

"You couldn't have come back to say hi?" Lou muttered, and Lyla felt like crawling under the table.

"Communication goes both ways. He could have written, but he chose not to. I didn't close the door on our relationship," Mason said, and Lou held up her hands defensively.

"But we didn't deserve to be punished because you fought with Dad," Kevin told him. The hurt in his voice threatened to break Lyla's heart.

Mason stared at his brother, and shook his head with a sigh. "I wasn't punishing you. I wanted to see you – all of you. But even when I tried to write in the beginning, Dad wouldn't respond. I couldn't fight any more, and if I came back I wouldn't have left again." It was the first time Lyla had seen him upset, or at least without the help of alcohol.

"Was it worth it? Not seeing us? I'm your brother and I barely know you," Kevin shot at him. Lyla instinctively placed her hand over his, surprised when he let her.

Mason scrubbed his face with his hands, and Lyla feared he would get up from the table to avoid the conversation.

"I wish I hadn't had to make a decision between my life and family, but Dad made that decision for me. You were too young to understand, and I was too young to think of what my leaving would do to our family—"

"But it was worth it," Mrs Klaus interjected for him.

Mason, and the rest of the table, stared at her in wonder.

"You wouldn't be the man you are now if you hadn't gone, and this lovely lady wouldn't be sitting with us. We can't change the past. We have each other now, and that's all that matters," she insisted.

A silence descended.

"It's a good thing you get to witness the crazy before you walk down the aisle," Kevin said in a hushed tone, nudging Lyla, and she didn't know what to say. She didn't think they were crazy; she thought they were a family who loved each other very much.

"Enough, Kevin!" Mason said, before looking to his mother. "To answer your earlier question, so we can put this topic to bed: what Frederick wants or doesn't want is of no concern to me. We went before the council as requested. They asked their questions, Lyla answered, and we left."

"Did they ask you what your decision will be?" Mrs Klaus asked, though she didn't look up from her dessert. Lyla guessed she was too nervous.

"They can ask as much or as little as they want. I don't know yet," Mason answered. Wiping his lips with a napkin, he rose from the table.

"I don't want to press you, but—" Mrs Klaus said, but Mason was already pushing in his chair. He kissed her on the side of the head, silencing her.

"I'm going to feed the reindeer. Kevin, since you're so eager to get to know me, you can help me," Mason said, motioning for his brother to join him.

Kevin groaned, but Lyla caught a sly smile as he got up and took their dishes.

Mrs Klaus sighed as her sons left. "I think I'm going to have an early night," she said. "There's some food for Sara in the dishes in the fridge."

She left looking ten years older than when they had

first sat down to eat. Lyla couldn't imagine the stress she was under, trying to help run the village, grieve for her husband, and try to get her son to stay. It would be too much for anyone.

"Can I ask what the seat *is*?" she asked Lou once they were alone and the table was cleared. "I don't really understand what a Klaus does."

"They lead the council and oversee the village," Lou said. "Think of it as like a president or a king – or queen," she added, sounding more uncertain.

"Not so much about a red suit and a sack of presents then?"

Lou burst out laughing. "No, that's more of a team job. The sleigh drivers, those who deliver the gifts to the outside world, number more than fifty. You can't expect one person to get around the whole world in one night!"

Lyla didn't expect even fifty people to be able to get around the whole world in one night.

"And you're in charge of the sleighs?" she asked, desperate for clarity.

"Yes, I train the drivers and make sure the sleighs are maintained. Sara manages the engineering department, and we've made some advancements lately that will speed up our deliveries, but the new tech is wreaking havoc on the old system."

Lyla could offer her nothing but a puzzled frown. *Sleigh technology?*

"Not that you need to worry about any of that," Lou promised.

That was a relief. "So, Mason wouldn't have to do anything on Christmas Eve?"

"It's our busiest night – he would oversee the whole operation," Lou explained, "he would make sure everything gets to where it's supposed to be at the right time."

Lyla was slightly frustrated about the lack of details. *What's 'everything'?* She assumed it was presents, but considering she had been wrong about so many other things, she wasn't sure.

"Are you happy working with the sleighs? You could have taken your father's place. Your mum mentioned something before..."

Lou reared back, waving her hands. "I'm happy where I am. I used to get in trouble sleigh racing; being the best driver then allows me to teach others now. The eldest is supposed to accept the role, but I never truly wanted it. After my accident, I wasn't going to do anything in this life I didn't want to, and I make sure the sleigh workshop is safe so that what happened to me won't happen again," she said firmly, moving away from the table and towards the fridge.

"Did Mason want to become Klaus, before or after you declined?" Lyla asked, leaning against the kitchen counter.

"He did, and even Dad knew Mason would be the better fit. He loves micromanaging, and he was great with all the workers and the council. The issue between them was that there were many things Mason wanted to do first."

"And he wasn't allowed?"

"There's more to it than that. You'd have to talk to him about it."

Lyla nodded, understanding Lou's desire to protect her brother's secrets.

Lou took the dishes from the fridge and placed them on her lap. "I sensed some distance between the two of you this evening. Don't let the council frighten you. They might seem scary, but they're all just terrified that Yule will one day be exposed."

"Are you?" Lyla asked, wondering if everyone in Yule wanted it to be kept a secret.

"Scared of exposure?" Lou nodded. "I think it's inevitable – but I also think it's a waste of time worrying about something that might or might not happen." They headed to the front door. "Mum!" she called up the stairs.

"Lou! Are you going? I'm hopping in the bath. Make sure to take the food in the fridge. I added some apple crumble, since Sara doesn't like rhubarb," Mrs Klaus called down, and Lyla smiled. Even with everything going on, Mrs Klaus still thought of others and their needs.

"She'll love it! I'll see you in the morning!" Lou shouted with a chuckle before turning back to Lyla.

"I wish I could tell you all my brother's secrets to help you figure him out. But to be honest, I haven't got a clue. This decision he has to make is going to bring up his past, and he needs someone to support him."

"He has you and an entire village," Lyla said.

"True, but I get the feeling he wouldn't have brought you here if it wasn't to have you in his corner," Lou said as Lyla opened the door for her.

She had a point. *Maybe he wanted me here because I didn't know him back then? I can't judge him for the past.*

Once Lou was gone, Lyla found peace in the comfort of her room. The thought of Mason being anything like a president made her laugh. He certainly had the stoic nature down pat. Still, she couldn't imagine him leaving all he had built for himself in the outside world to come back here.

With the door closed behind her, she threw herself down on the bed, and caught sight of the drawer Mason had taken the ring from. Suddenly the memory of the kiss flooded back, and she buried her face in the duvet and let out a small scream. Remembering the feel of his lips, how she had misunderstood and kissed him back, only furthered her humiliation, her cheeks flaring hot. She wished

Lou had told her more about why Mason had left in the first place – why he was the way he was. One minute she saw a glimpse of his heart, and the next a mask descended. She needed to clear her mind and put some distance between them – because she could still feel the lingering sensation of his lips on hers.

It meant nothing; it was a kiss, she assured herself, getting ready for bed. *He just didn't want to be caught in the middle of an argument.* Sleeping in his oversized sweatshirt did nothing to ease her mind, but the one thing they had forgotten to buy was pyjamas. She usually slept in T-shirts, but she didn't want to do that here in case someone, especially Mason, came in unexpectantly.

But what if that wasn't the only reason? What he said in the hall about loving me... did he mean it? He couldn't. But the way he talked about the staff, and my love for the company... Could he really invent it so easily?

Before Lyla had a chance to get her thoughts in order, she heard the soft click of the door opening and closing. Jones, who had been curled up beside her, leapt off the bed. Startled, she sat up and turned on the light beside her to find Mason lingering by the door.

"You scared the shit out of me. If you're here to talk, I'm not in the mood," she said, yanking the covers up to hide her chest.

He had a glint in his eye. "My bad. I was thinking we could carry on where we left off in the town square."

She tossed the blanket at the end of the bed at him pathetically. It was that or the lamp, and since it looked like an antique, she didn't want to upset Mrs Klaus by destroying it.

He caught it easily. "Only trying to lighten the mood. I thought you would be asleep by now." The traitorous

Jones was at his feet, purring happily until he was picked up and returned to the bed.

"And you thought it would be okay to creep into my room – half-naked, I might add?" She tried not to stare at his bare chest, though something so magnificent deserved to be seen. She silenced that thought as Jones distracted her by rubbing his head against her.

"My brother caught me coming back from the bathroom before I went into one of the spare rooms. I told him you were using the en suite, and I couldn't exactly return to the spare room without him asking a thousand questions," he explained.

She nodded, but before she could offer him the long seat at the end of the bed, he was already lying down beside her.

"You can take the floor!" she hissed, moving further away.

"It's only for one night," he said, leaning on his elbows. "Or can you not resist me?"

She smacked him with a pillow. "The floor should suit you fine."

"It's freezing on the floor. Even the damn cat isn't sleeping on it. If you don't want to sleep with me, then *you* can take the floor."

Lyla glared at the carpet. "I'm not sleeping on the floor. This is my room!" she argued, though that wasn't technically true.

"Then stop being precious and go to sleep," he said, turning his back to her.

She noticed the sparse freckles on his shoulders. Learning intimate details like this about him was stirring something in her she didn't want to address.

"I'm not being precious," she muttered, and tried to

pull more of the duvet to her side, hoping he would suffer in the cold.

"Yes you are." He gave one sharp pull; taken by surprise, Lyla rolled onto the floor. Her hip hit the ground first, and she groaned in pain.

"MASON!" she shouted, not caring if she woke the house.

A devilishly handsome smile attached to a smug face popped over the side of the bed.

"Wouldn't have happened if you had shared like a normal person. Maybe you really are concerned that you can't keep your hands to yourself, and that's why you insist on hogging the covers." Mason offered her a hand, but she slapped it away and got to her feet.

"The only place I'm touching you is in your dreams," she retorted, resting her hands on the bed and staring him down.

His smirk made her take a pillow and smack him with it until he backed up to his side of the bed. Once he was off her side, she checked her hip to see a nice bruise forming and groaned again in irritation.

"Moan any louder, and everyone will hear us," he said, and she suddenly realised what he meant.

"Stop talking to me."

"I'm only thinking of your modesty. Moaning in my room might give them ideas."

"You flung me off the bed!"

Once a pillow fort was secured between them, she climbed under the duvet. He sighed.

"Don't say anything," she snapped, and he chuckled softly before turning away from her.

With her back to him, she cradled the pillow. *How the hell did I go from hating his guts to sharing his bed in a winter wonderland? I would like to wake up from this nightmare now.*

"Lyla?" he whispered.

"What, Mason?" His name slipped easily from her lips. She wasn't sure when he'd gone from Klaus to Mason in her mind, but hearing it aloud filled the air with a tension that she was sure neither of them were ready to address.

"Goodnight," he said, and the softness of his tone took her by surprise.

"Goodnight," she grumbled, before closing her eyes and drifting off.

CHAPTER THIRTEEN

"You can't leave me alone! What was the point in bringing me, only to leave me with your family?!"

Lyla was still angry at Mason for the kiss and the lies, but also at herself for waking up cradled in his arms – and for how much she hadn't wanted to leave the embrace. For the first time in days, she'd actually felt safe... in the arms of the person who'd put her in danger.

"Because if you're here, then I don't have to be, and I can work in peace while you distract them," Mason argued, making the bed with military efficiency. They were both dressed and had been up a while, though few words had been exchanged.

"Lie to them, you mean," she muttered. "If we're hardly together, how are we supposed to play the doting couple—?"

"You didn't seem to care about appearances when you

were giving me the silent treatment during last night's dinner!"

A knock on the bedroom door cut them off. "Mason! Are you decent? I told the committee you'll help set up the gingerbread house competition happening this evening!"

Mason opened the door.

"I've got to be at the workshop all day; a shipment is coming down from the mountain. I was going to take Lyla with me, but she'd probably be bored. There's more paperwork than I care to admit for me to get through. Mum, I don't have time for the festivities."

Lyla made herself snuggle close to him. "I thought you wanted to spend some time together, sweetie! I have so much to learn..." She pinched him, and he visibly struggled to maintain his composure.

"I didn't realise you already had plans," Mrs Klaus said, sounding disappointed. "Lyla does have a lot to learn and so much to see, but the committee could use another volunteer."

Kevin, passing in the hallway, said, "Dad always had time," which only made Lyla feel guilty.

"Well, Dad was a lot more organised than I am," Mason retorted. Lyla didn't believe that for a minute. Mason was the most detail-orientated person she had ever met.

"I can help!" she found herself offering.

"Are you sure you don't mind?" asked Mrs Klaus, though her smile gave away her excitement.

"Of course she doesn't." Mason planted an exaggerated kiss on Lyla's cheek. "Be good!"

She allowed herself to be led away by Mrs Klaus, but not before she trod on his foot, making him yelp in a most undignified way. She suppressed a laugh. She hadn't thought he was even capable of such a sound.

"Come with me into the village, and I can introduce

you around. We need help setting up for this evening and making sure every stall has the ingredients and equipment it needs," Mrs Klaus said.

Sounds easy enough, Lyla thought.

In the village square, a grand stage with numerous kitchen stations had been set up. The lamp posts were decorated with gingerbread-house-covered banners advertising the competition. Lyla was intimidated by the sheer scale of it all.

"Are you sure you want to do this? I don't wish to overwhelm you," Mrs Klaus said.

Lyla nodded, wrapping her coat around herself. "It's only a gingerbread house competition – it's hardly rocket science." She hoped.

"The local school painted the backdrop," Mrs Klaus told her as they walked along the stage while workers fluttered around them on the snow-shovelled paths. Ovens and tables were being set up in rows. Lyla wondered how the event would continue if it snowed, but she figured they must be prepared for something so likely.

"They did a great job," she answered, looking at the painted gingerbread house; though it was slightly tilted, it was perfect for the event. She was happy to finally feel useful – until she noticed Natalie from the dress shop coming towards them. *Bloody hell, I can't even walk in heels on a normal road without falling over! Anyone who wears heels on cobbled paths is taking their own life in their hands.*

"Natalie!" Mrs Klaus beamed. "How good of you to help. Your mum said you had volunteered, though I didn't expect you so early."

"The school term is finished, so I thought I would lend a hand, since everyone is so busy," Natalie said, embracing Mrs Klaus. Lyla resisted the urge to roll her eyes. Mason's ex-girlfriend was dressed to perfection in a wrap dress and long overcoat, and Lyla couldn't help but feel inferior, considering she was dressed in more layers than a yeti – but then again, they were used to this climate, whereas she still feared losing a limb to frostbite.

"If there's anything else you need during this time, please don't hesitate to let me know. I can only imagine how hard this is for you," Natalie continued, pretending Lyla didn't exist.

"Thank you, but I haven't a moment to think on it – and Lyla's arrival has certainly brightened up the whole house." From Mrs Klaus' side glance, it hadn't escaped her notice that Natalie hadn't addressed her presence. "Would you be a dear and work together – show Lyla what needs to be done? I have to get to the council for a meeting on the gala," she said, before being called away by a group on the other side of the stage.

The two of them were left in an awkward silence. The last thing Lyla wanted was to be ordered about by Natalie, but since it would make Mrs Klaus' day a little easier, she was obliged to listen – and if they were busy, at least they wouldn't have to speak.

Natalie surprised her by taking her hands and pulling her in close. "Now that we're alone, please tell me how they are really doing? I do worry about them all," she whispered.

"They're doing fine. I'm sure once the season ends it will be harder for them, but I think they welcome the distraction," Lyla said, trying to take back custody of her hands, but the woman was determined to keep her hold.

"It hurts me so much that there's such a distance between us now, but that's the way life works." Natalie was looking at her as though she was the cause of said distance, and the not-so-gentle squeeze of her hand only confirmed it.

Lyla ignored that, seeing a rare opportunity to learn more about Mason's past. "You were close to the family? You said before that you and Mason were childhood friends?"

Natalie released her hands, only to slap her lightly on the arm. "Childhood friends – that would be putting it mildly. Since we're friends now..." She paused for a minute to ascertain that they were alone on the stage. "I think I can tell you, and I don't think Mason would mind me informing you, that we were engaged before he left."

Lyla felt her stomach hit the floor. *He was engaged before he left? He was so young! And a warning that I might be ambushed by the jilted fiancée would have been nice.*

"Engaged? Surely he broke it off before he left?" The question flew out before she could stop herself.

"Yes, we were, and yes, he did break it off. Rather abruptly, I might add. Of course, I've forgiven him. We'd been together since school, so his family became a second to my own. You can understand why I'm so worried about them," Natalie told her, unboxing what looked like equipment for each competitor to use later. "If you want to start unboxing, that would be a great help." Clearly, she had finished divulging information.

They worked in silence, setting up the cooking equipment, ingredients and tools, and laying out clipboards for the judges. It wasn't long before they were finished, and a flustered Mrs Klaus appeared on the stage.

"Two of our contestants have dropped out! They're too busy at the workshop, and with the sleighs needing more work, Lou can't spare them!" she exclaimed.

Lyla thought, *I don't blame them*. Baking wasn't her

favourite activity at the best of times, but doing it in front of people and competing with others sounded like her worst nightmare.

"Oh no!" she said aloud. "What a shame."

Natalie looked over at her, and then said brightly, "Why don't you and I fill in for them, Lyla? I'm sure that would be a huge relief for Edith."

Lyla panicked. "I really don't think that's a good idea. I'd like to help, but for the safety of everyone involved I shouldn't be around an oven," she gabbled, though it only seemed to spur Natalie on.

"There's no need to be modest. We'll give you everything you need. We would be more than happy to fill in," Natalie announced, and Lyla groaned internally. She could hardly boil water.

"Baking isn't my strong suit. Maybe there's something else I can—"

"Don't be silly! It's all for fun and charity – the school needs a new theatre. The villagers bid on their favourites, and the highest bid is the winner. There are instructions for every step. It'll be easy, and how wonderful for everyone to see the new Mrs Klaus embracing our traditions," Natalie rattled on.

"I wouldn't want you to feel any pressure," Mrs Klaus chimed in, though the relief in her eyes at having the positions filled weighed on Lyla. *There's no way I'm getting out of this.*

She gritted her teeth. "I thrive on pressure. And I can hardly refuse when the kids need a new theatre!"

"I'll sign us up." Natalie wandered off.

Lyla couldn't believe she was going to compete in a baking competition – and against Ms Perfect! She wished Mason was here to see it; he wouldn't be able to contain his amusement.

"Are you sure you're okay with this?" Mrs Klaus asked, taking her arm.

"What's a bit of friendly competition? I'll try not to embarrass you too much."

"The fact you were willing to help at all is prize enough," Mrs Klaus offered, but Lyla had made up her mind. The last thing she wanted to do was lose to Mason's ex in front of the entire village. Luckily she had a few hours before it started to plan Natalie's defeat.

Lyla was immensely grateful for the instructions. There were contestants of every age, so they were simple, and she'd finished baking sooner than she'd expected. Unfortunately, she only had a few minutes to finish decorating, though she was still trying to construct the damn thing. She was realising that she *didn't* thrive under pressure, or at least not when icing was involved.

Natalie, however, was having no such issues. Her gingerbread house seemed to be coming together effortlessly. She didn't look the least bit fazed, not a perfect hair out of place, while Lyla was sure she looked like a frazzled mess. Lyla's gingerbread was also distinctly uneven; some pieces were too pale and didn't look like they'd support much weight, while others were slightly burnt.

The base should be solid enough, she thought, trying to keep her walls standing. The walls were certainly thick enough, but that only made her worry she had used too much dough. She had also used almost half the jar of dried ginger when the cap broke off, so she was sure it was inedible. She didn't care about winning; she merely wanted to finish to save some face in front of the insufferably cheerful Natalie.

"I didn't think I'd ever see you in an apron, let alone in a baking competition," Mason said, frightening her as he came up behind her, clipboard in his hand. His smile distracted her from her work. In the office, he was always so uptight; seeing him relaxed was like seeing a new person – a person she didn't entirely hate.

"I thought you didn't have time to come, and there are plenty of things you don't know about me," she said, adding far too much icing to the walls she was trying to fuse together.

"The whole office knows what a terrible cook you are. I'm surprised *you* weren't the one who set it alight."

She scowled at the reminder of the mishap that had landed her here. "So, are you here merely to mock me and my incompetence?"

"No. Lou had to bow out of judging to help repair the sleigh's engine, and since a Klaus has always been a judge, I didn't have much of a choice but to offer to step in – especially when I heard my dear wife-to-be was taking part," he said, leaning on the counter.

"Don't you think it's unfair to have you be a judge? But since I definitely can't win, be sure to bid on my house and save your dear fiancée the embarrassment."

"Absolutely – though I think we'll have to feed it to the wolves, because no human should eat such a creation." They both examined the slightly burnt and tilted structure, the icing already dripping down the sides because she'd applied it too soon after it came out of the oven.

"Mason! Can you come and give me a hand?" Natalie called, and Lyla resisted the urge to roll her eyes. *What could she possibly need help with?*

"I'll be right over," he said, though he made no effort to move.

"Don't let me keep you. I'm sure *Natalie's* is perfect – and edible," she said sweetly, though her irritation caused her to break off the arm of a gingerbread man by accident. *If it had been a competition about advertising spreadsheets, I would have kicked her arse.*

"Are you jealous?" Mason asked, moving behind her, and she turned to face him. She didn't want Natalie to think they were talking about her.

"Nope," she said, offering him the broken gingerbread arm. She was surprised when he popped it in his mouth without any hesitation. "I would hate for you to suffer my baking while hers is so perfect," she muttered.

He chewed, then was unable to hide his disgust at the taste. Lyla stifled a laugh, watching him struggle to swallow.

"You did that on purpose," he accused, his hands on either side of her, trapping her against the counter. His gaze made Lyla flush. She needed him to leave before she destroyed her hard work out of sheer frustration.

"Don't you have other people to judge? I wouldn't want to keep you from those who deserve your attention. I have a house to decorate, and you're blocking me from getting to my icing."

He released her with a chuckle and looked down at the piping bag of white icing leaking out onto the counter.

"Excuse me. I won't keep you from decorating," he said, offering it to her, and she snatched it from him.

Once he had moved on, she looked up to see that the timer was ticking down. She had got most of it in place, but she still needed to put the gumdrops on, and the final wall wouldn't stand on its own. Natalie, across from her, had already finished and was watching her with a bemused smile. Lyla didn't know why she was so determined to beat her; it was only a stupid gingerbread house.

She licked the icing from her fingers as the wall finally stood on its own, seconds before the final timer rang. She sighed in relief as the judges started to come around.

"So glad you finished in time – you were cutting it close," Natalie called in an astonished tone that made Lyla want to flatten her. "I really thought you weren't going to make it. Every house is auctioned for charity, so it's important that each one gets made."

"It's a good thing I finished then—" Lyla began, only to feel her throat suddenly tighten. She froze.

"Are you okay? You look flushed," Natalie said hesitantly.

Lyla's tongue was tingling. She glanced at the angry rash spreading across her hands.

"Lyla, what is it?" Natalie asked.

"Get Mason!" she rasped, clutching her chest, but Natalie only stood there, watching in alarm as the rash spread up her neck. Lyla shoved past her and into the crowd watching the competition to the judges' table, where she saw Mason and Mrs Klaus. She collapsed at his feet.

He bent down to her, panic-stricken. "Lyla, what the fuck happened?"

"Strawberries," she rasped, struggling to breathe.

Mason blanched at her words. He lifted her into his arms.

"Don't panic. I've got you," he said, carrying her away from the watching crowd. "The doctor isn't far from here – hold on."

Lyla could hear the fear in his voice as he ran down the lanes. The burn in her chest intensified as they went, and she could no longer fight the overwhelming urge to close her eyes.

CHAPTER FOURTEEN

When Lyla woke, she was back in bed.

The weight of the sheets was comforting, although a little stifling after such a shock. The last thing she remembered was collapsing at Mason's feet. Her head was groggy and she felt exhausted, though her chest was no longer tight and the hives were gone from her skin. She didn't know what she had been given, but it seemed to have helped her allergy much more effectively than anything back home. She tried to place her hand on her chest, only to realise that Mason, sleeping beside her, had hold of it. With her free hand, she took her glasses from the nightstand, relieved they hadn't been lost in the chaos. The clock told her it was already 6pm. She couldn't believe she had slept through the night and well into the next day.

Slowly, she remembered him carrying her in his arms. The panic in his eyes and the way he'd called her name, trying to keep her awake until she passed out. With her free hand, she brushed his blonde hair from his face. Her finger traced his cheek, his nose, his lips... she wanted to lean forward and kiss him, if only to thank him for saving her life, but as she studied his features, Natalie's words sprang to the forefront of her mind. *They were engaged before he left. Engaged. Why bring me here when there was someone who clearly hadn't given up on him still waiting?* She suddenly felt like she was part of a game she didn't understand.

Slipping her hand out of his, she left him to sleep. It was only when she reached for the doorknob that she realised her ring was missing. She clenched her hand in a fist, remembering she had placed it in a dish on the counter when she was making the gingerbread house. *I left it behind,* she fretted. *It might still be there. Maybe Mason has it, or someone could have found it and returned it to the house while I slept.* She wished she had never taken it off, or that she had never agreed to bake the damn gingerbread house in the first place.

"Lyla! Thank goodness you're awake. Are you feeling better? I don't know how it could have happened! I specifically told Natalie not to put any strawberry icing or ingredients with any traces of it on your stand," Mrs Klaus babbled when Lyla joined her in the kitchen. Her words totally wiped away any thoughts of the missing ring.

She knew about my allergy? That bitch tried to kill me! I didn't even use strawberry icing... she must have put some in the vanilla. Lyla kept the thought to herself. There was no way to prove it, and it was obvious the woman was close to the family. *The stupid woman probably wanted to mess with me and didn't realise how severe my reaction would be.*

"Much better, thank you. I should have been more careful."

"A terrible accident, but what a relief you're all right! Natalie was beside herself – said she had meant to take the icing to her own station, but with everything going on, she exchanged hers for yours," Mrs Klaus fussed.

"You'd never have known from the bags – mine certainly looked plain. I couldn't even taste it," Lyla muttered. "It's understandable she made such a mistake," she assured Mrs Klaus, trying to sound brighter. She didn't want to start accusing people of attempted murder in a village away from the rest of the world. *Do they even have a police force, or do the council decide everything?* It was another question she didn't have the energy to ask.

"An honest mistake," Mrs Klaus agreed. "The doctor gave Mason a tonic for you to drink once you were up and about, in case you start to feel ill again. We didn't expect you to sleep so long – we were worried."

"Thank you. I'll keep that in mind. I don't tend to suffer recurrence, and it was such a small amount. It was probably the shock that knocked me out for so long," Lyla said, not wanting to make a fuss. She wanted to forget the matter had even happened. If she had had such a reaction at home she would be suffering for a few days. But whatever the doctor had given her left her feeling almost normal. It was the lingering anxiety that remained. *I'll stay away from Natalie from now on. Hopefully, she'll do the same. At least she was smart enough to make up a lie about it.*

"Let's put it behind us, and have a nice dinner," Mrs Klaus said, returning to her cooking.

"Is there anything I can do to help? But please be warned, I haven't helped anyone cook since my mum passed away – and even then what we made was often burnt or tasteless. We usually ended up ordering pizza," Lyla confessed, then cringed slightly at the overshare. She took the lid off one of the pots on the stove; the steam fogged up her glasses, but the smell was tantalising. Her mouth watered, though she didn't think her body was ready for a hearty meal.

"You can't be that bad. You did well with the gingerbread house," Mrs Klaus said encouragingly.

"Did you taste it?" Lyla asked, and Mrs Klaus hesitated.

"The ginger was... quite intense, but you persevered, which is a trait I greatly admire – and one you will need if you marry my son." She winked, offering Lyla an apron with a snowman basking in the summer sun on the front. "How about something simple? You can prep the vegetables. I don't think you can do much harm there."

"Do you want the Brussels sprouts whole or sliced in two?" Lyla asked. Mrs Klaus was working from a handwritten cookbook bound in leather that looked older than Mrs Klaus herself. Lyla wanted to put as much care into her job as Mrs Klaus put into everything she weighed and sliced.

"Throw them in whole – no need to be too precious about it," Mrs Klaus said as Kevin came in and took a seat at the counter.

"What's cooking? I'm starving!"

Lyla realised he was still wearing the same clothes from yesterday. "Have you been to bed?" she asked, seeing the dark rings around his eyes.

"Not yet. I was working on a design for a new Christmas game – evil elves take over the world," he told her, his face lighting up.

"Sounds like a bestseller," Lyla said, and it really did. She would have bought it for her own company, if they dealt in games.

He shrugged, taking an energy drink from the fridge. "I think so. Suppose I should ask how you are. Heard you almost died?"

Lyla was surprised and delighted that he was actually trying to prolong a conversation with her. "An allergic reaction, but it takes a lot more than a bag of icing to get rid of me," she said.

He looked impressed.

"I'm sure Natalie will be disappointed," he replied with a knowing look, and Lyla winked at him. *He might be a bratty teen, but it's obvious he's smart and observant to what's happening around him.*

"Food won't be ready for another hour. I suggest you take a rest. You had an awful fright yesterday," Mrs Klaus told Lyla, taking the drink from Kevin's hand and shooing him out from under their feet. "How the boy survives on next to no sleep is a wonder – one day I'll find him passed out under the tree," she added, though Lyla could tell she was proud of him.

"Probably his way of coping. I couldn't sleep for months after my mum passed," she said without thinking, and the older woman stopped mid-chop. "Sorry, I didn't mean..."

"I didn't think of that," Mrs Klaus confessed. "I've been trying to give him his space, and if designing those games is what brings him some peace, then I try not to intervene. He had less time with Henry compared to the others." She sniffled, placing a tray of Lyla's chopped vegetables into the oven for roasting.

"Any time is better than none. He has all of you to keep Mr Klaus's memory alive – I only wish I had had that," Lyla said.

Mrs Klaus seemed comforted by her words. "Don't you have any other family?"

"No," Lyla said, a little too quickly. "I mean, my dad is alive, but he's currently on wife number four, and I was raised by nannies in my mother's old townhouse. I don't think he ever got over the loss; he's been trying to replace her ever since. I was a reminder."

She couldn't believe she was admitting so much to a near stranger, but she reminded herself that she wouldn't see these people after a couple more days, so it didn't matter what she did or didn't say.

"To grow up alone... I'm sorry you had to grieve by yourself," Mrs Klaus said with a sympathetic smile.

"I had my grandfather, who visited me as often as he could when he wasn't managing the company – so I grew up in the company. I got to know everyone, from the office to the warehouse. It wasn't a complete misery," Lyla said, not wanting the pity.

"I'm sure your mum would be very proud of the young woman you have become," Mrs Klaus said, placing a hand on her shoulder.

Lyla went to throw the peelings in the bin, feeling her eyes prickle with tears, even as her chest swelled with joy. It was the first time anyone had said such a thing to her. She hoped Mrs Klaus was right; it was all she had ever wanted.

CHAPTER FIFTEEN

The clock on the bedside table read 2:59am, which Lyla guessed was roughly 12pm back home. She knew she would be exhausted by morning, but she was too wide awake after her post-reaction sleep to even consider bed now. While Mason slept, she wondered what she could do to repay him for saving her life.

The only thing she could think to do was tidy his father's side of the office. There was a distance between him and his mother, and she hoped sharing the space might help mend their relationship. Selfishly, it also meant he wouldn't be able to keep escaping to the workshop and leaving her in abject boredom for hours; this way, he could bring work home and spend more time with his family.

She took Jones with her, so Mason wouldn't be disturbed, and the chunky cat was happy to snuggle up by the fire while she got to work dusting and organising the files and drawers.

After a few hours, she was finally satisfied with her efforts. It had been hard work, but seeing all the scrolls and books organised, the desk clear of clutter and papers, was worth it. When the clock rang for 7am throughout the house, there wasn't a speck of dust left on the mantlepiece or the ornaments adorning it. She hadn't meant to stay up until morning, but she'd got carried away. Her back ached, and she was ready for food and a nap, but she was determined to show Mason what she had done first.

Padding down the hall to the kitchen, she found him at the breakfast table and beamed. Eagerly, she took his arm and dragged him away from the tense silence and bacon.

"Follow me," she said, excited to show him the new office.

He obeyed in confusion until they reached the room. She swung open the doors and showed off the dust- and clutter-free room, elated.

"Ta-da! Welcome to your new workspace."

His face fell as he stepped into the room. *Not the immediate reaction I was expecting...* Mason went to his father's desk, where there were no longer papers stacked high and strewn all over the place.

"What did you do?" he asked quietly, looking at the organised room. Not a book or scroll was out of place.

"What are you talking about? I thought I would clean it up, make it nice for your mum. I don't think anyone's had a chance to clean it in a while."

"What business is it of yours what state my father's office is in? What were you doing in here?" he snapped.

Taken aback, she said, "I had to send an email the other day, and your mum said it wasn't an issue. I didn't go in without asking. I thought you could use the desk to work so you could spend more time with your family instead of going to the workshop."

He was too busy staring at the clean desk to look at her. "You had permission to send an email, not to rearrange his desk! This was his life!"

She hadn't expected him to be so upset. Though she knew it was his grief speaking, hurt overwhelmed her. She hadn't meant to overstep, but then she thought of how she would have felt if someone had gone into her mum's paints without permission. She cursed herself for getting carried away.

"I'm sorry. I promise everything is organised in the drawers – I didn't throw anything out. I thought I was doing something nice to thank you for the clothes and saving my life," she explained.

His features creased as he looked through the papers organised on the desk, before rifling through the drawers frantically. "Where is the List?" he demanded, coming towards her, and she took a step back.

"What list?" she asked, trying to remain calm. Even in anger, she knew he wouldn't hurt her.

"THE List," he snarled. "It was on the desk. I put it there myself for Mum to look over. We can't have Christmas without the List. You have no idea what you've done!"

Lyla remembered the scroll with the names; he was talking about the naughty or nice list. Ignoring his glare, she pushed past him to climb the ladder where all the scrolls were placed. She found the new space she'd created for the next decade and grabbed the scroll, thrusting it into his hands once they were face to face again.

"Your damn list!" she snapped, though tears were threatening to spill over.

His eyes were on her hand. "Where is your ring?" he demanded.

"What?" she asked, confused.

"The ring I gave you. Where is it?" He grasped her hand in his, but she snatched it back.

"You don't have it?" she asked, covering her hand with the other.

"Why would I have *your* ring?"

Her stomach dropped. "I took it off during the competition. I thought someone might have found it and returned it!"

"You left a family heirloom in a dish?" he seethed.

"I didn't mean to lose it! It was in a small dish beside the oven. I can get it back!" she babbled, but he wouldn't meet her eye. "I'm sorry! I'm sorry about the ring, and about moving the list. I didn't think—"

"No, you didn't. You never think," he said coldly.

She didn't know what to say. She had meant to do a good thing, and instead she only widened the distance between them.

When she didn't move, he went on. "You think you can do whatever you want, whenever you want. I thought you'd learnt from the office fire that there are consequences for your actions. This was my father's space, and if I wanted to use it I would have. Leave before I say something I'll regret!"

"I know you're grieving, but when you calm down, you'll regret your words," she choked out, and ran out of the office, not wanting to look at him.

Desperate to get away from him, she fled to the only sanctuary she could think of – her bedroom. She walked as fast as she could, afraid she would be stopped by Mrs Klaus or Kevin. If she could close the door behind her for a minute and bury her face in Jones's fur, she could at least pretend that she wasn't here.

She stumbled into the room, but Jones's chair was

empty. Horror swept through her. *The office door! I left it open when I ran out.*

"Jones!" she called desperately, knowing he would never come. He was a cat. She dashed to look over the bannisters and found the front door wide open, and Kevin carrying in logs for the fireplaces.

"Kevin! The door! Did you see Jones?" she gasped. Kevin looked confused as he took off his headphones, and then turned pale when they both registered the paw prints in the snow alongside his.

"Sorry – I didn't realise he was out of your room. I was coming in and out, so I left the door open," he said, dropping the logs. Lyla was already hurrying down the stairs. "You can't go out there alone – wait here! I'll go get Mason!"

She didn't answer that; the last thing she wanted was another scolding. She pulled on her shoes and jacket and ran past Kevin and out of the house.

"Damn it, Jones!" she hissed, moving as fast as she could in ankle-deep snow after the prints. Before she knew it, she could no longer see the road or where she was headed in the thick woods behind the house. Shrouded in darkness, all she could see was a few feet ahead. The lack of light forced her to bend over in order to make out the small paw prints.

"Jones!" she called into the darkness, zipping up her jacket against the increasing wind. She couldn't think of returning, or the fear of the cold.

The paw prints came to an end as she reached what looked like a hollow trunk.

"Jones?" she repeated softly, crouching to look inside, where she saw the glint of his eyes. Her breath heaved in relief as she reached into the trunk and gently pulled him free.

"Why did you run off?" she asked, kissing his damp, furry head. He was shaking; she tucked him inside her jacket.

When she straightened up, fear streaked down her spine. She had no idea which way she had come, and it was growing darker. Stooping down, she followed her footprints. Thanks to the dense trees, the accumulation of snow had slowed.

"You had to pick today of all days to run away," Lyla said through chattering teeth, grateful for the heat the cat was providing. She stilled, trying to figure out which direction to go. She'd been too focused on his paw prints to notice anything like markings on trees. Taking a deep, painfully cold breath, she chose a path when she felt eyes on her.

"Mason? Kevin?" she called, praying they had come after her. *Kevin saw me run off and went to get Mason. As angry as he is at me, he won't let me freeze to death.* She took a few steps towards the sound... and found sets of luminous blue eyes staring back at her.

"Wolves. Fucking wolves," she muttered, the cold freezing her breath. She backed up slowly, but the growls echoed from behind her. She glanced over her shoulder, greeted by two more sets of eyes. "Can my day get *any* worse?"

"Lyla! Lyla, call out if you can hear me!"

Her eyes snapped to the trees; she couldn't see anyone, but that was Mason in the near distance. She opened her mouth, but she was too paralysed to cry out. The wolves crept forward, teeth bared, and she was sure one word from her would bait the animals to attack. Seeing them clearly, she didn't think wolves should be so large, their fur so white it almost hid them against the snow.

Jones tried to paw at her chest, sensing the danger, but she held him tight, not caring if she hurt him. If he ran, he would trigger an attack. The wolves formed a semi-circle, forcing her back; she attempted to put some distance between herself and the snarling beasts. Instead, she tripped over a log concealed by the snow.

She grunted loudly as her back hit the log and she landed in the snow. When she gathered her senses, a wolf stood on the log, peering down at her, saliva dripping from its jaws. Lyla closed her eyes, bracing herself for the attack – and a light flashed before her.

Flaming torch in hand, Mason knocked the wolf from the log. There was a yelp of pain, and the other wolves backed away from the flames.

"Get up!" Mason ordered, pulling her to her feet with his free hand. "We need to run. Follow the treeline behind you – keep straight and you'll come to a path." He spoke so quickly, she struggled to keep up. The wolves snarled and snapped, concealing themselves among the underbrush now that there was more than one human to take down. When Lyla didn't respond, Mason shoved her in the opposite direction of where he had come from.

"We can't outrun wolves," she argued, shivering. "Have you seen the size of them?" Her feet sank deeper into the snow the longer they waited. Her hands numbed by the cold, she didn't think she had the strength to fight if they attacked.

"Run or be their dinner. You passed the border. They know you're an outsider because your blood doesn't smell the same as ours," Mason snapped.

Dread overwhelmed her. "I'm not going to leave you here with them!"

"They won't attack me. Go before the fire goes out!" he shouted, gripping her collar and then shoving her again, causing her to stumble.

Another set of eyes appeared in the darkness, and his dimming torch was all the persuasion she needed. Lyla ran

– if it could even be called running through the ankle-deep snow. Clutching Jones made it even harder to keep her balance. She kept glancing over her shoulder, waiting for Mason to follow. Finally she saw him keeping pace not far behind her and could only pray the wolves wouldn't attack him in order to get to her.

The uphill climb levelled out, and she emerged from the trees onto a path. She braced her hands on her knees, the taste of blood wet in her mouth. *I really need to exercise more.*

"Don't stop – not until you're on the other side of the gate!" Mason shouted, approaching the treeline.

What gate!? Lyla thought, but as she looked up at the end of the path she saw it. Running came easier on the cleared path, but with numb fingers, she struggled with the rope tying the gate closed. She pulled as hard as she could at the knot, catching her breath as it unravelled. It finally opened as Mason reached her side. She was so focused on getting the gate open, she hadn't noticed the wolves close behind him.

Mason stopped to light the torches on either side of the gate; a wolf dived for him, and she was too slow to warn him. Her shout strangled in her throat as the beast's jaws clamped down on his arm. Mason cried out.

Before she could think about it, Lyla snatched the torch from the other side of the gate and cracked it over the head of the wolf. Loosening its jaw, the wolf dropped to the ground. Its packmates gathered around the fallen creature while Lyla dragged Mason to the other side of the gate and closed it.

"You're bleeding," she panted, though he probably already knew that.

"I'm fine, just a bite," Mason grunted, and they both turned to look at the wolves, who had suddenly remembered their prey. Lyla waited for them to jump the gate, but they stopped prowling forward when the torches flared brighter.

"Don't worry. They can't get past the gate – the fire will keep them back," Mason said. The relief nearly took her legs out from beneath her, though it sounded like he was in more pain than he wanted her to know.

"Are you sure?" she asked, kissing Jones's head as he popped up from inside her jacket. The wolves pacing in front of the gate did nothing to ease her fear.

"Let's get inside. There's meant to be a storm tonight, and once we're out of sight they'll give up the hunt," he told her. She was surprised when he took her hand and led her up the path to a log cabin. "My dad used to take us here to fish on the lake. No one's been here for a while." He lit the two torches outside the door.

"How are we going to get in?" she asked. Panicked, she noticed the blood dripping from his hand onto the snow.

"Got it covered." He winked, lifting a plant pot where a key sat.

How can he be so calm when he's bleeding and we just escaped death? She couldn't stop herself from shaking as he opened the door and ushered her inside.

The dark wood walls and stone fireplace were exactly what she considered a cabin should be. There was a couch with some cushions and a blanket, which looked inviting, but it was just as cold as outside. Mason was quick to find and light some candles, clearly having been here many times before. He placed them around the room while Lyla rubbed her arms, trying to warm herself as she stared out the windows to make sure there was no sign of the wolves. Ice crystals painted the glass, and the snow piled high on the windowsills obscured her view to the gate.

"Sit on the couch and catch your breath. I'll get a fire started," he said, noticing she was still by the door. Thankfully, the candles provided the light they needed to see each other clearly.

She was too cold to argue. The snow had already soaked through her jacket, so she stripped it off, and Jones was more than eager to jump out of her arms and settle on the couch.

"What were you thinking, running off into the woods? You could have been killed!" Mason added logs to the fire he had started. He was dripping blood everywhere, and the sight of it was freaking her out.

"I wasn't going to let Jones become their dinner – nor was I going to let him freeze to death."

He stared at her as she rushed into the kitchen and began to go through the cabinets like a mad woman. At least it was warming her up and using up the rest of her adrenaline.

"How did you find me? I could barely see my hand in front of my face out there." She found the first aid kit beneath the sink. However, her relief was short-lived: inside was only a nearly empty bottle of disinfectant and a single bandage. Luckily, there was a small bit of tape left on a roll to secure the bandage. It would have to do. She brought the box to Mason, standing by the fire. He took a step towards her. For a moment she thought he was going to kiss her, but then he stared down at her snow-covered boots.

"I followed your footprints," he informed her.

"Makes sense. Can you please sit down, because the blood is making me queasy," she said, forcing him to sit on the couch. Perching on the table in front of him, she opened the box.

"I didn't think you were the queasy type," he said, lifting his sleeve and exposing a row of small puncture wounds and two larger ones.

"I – was in an accident with my mum when I was a kid. Her blood was everywhere," she found herself admitting, and her chest swelled with grief. She hadn't thought about the day of the accident for the longest time. The details she had trained herself to forget.

"I'm sorry. I knew you lost your mum, but I didn't realise it was an accident," he said while she let some cotton wool absorb the disinfectant.

"This is going to hurt," she warned, applying it to his wounds. He hissed in pain. "Told you so." She cleaned away the blood. "Do you have shots here? I don't want you getting rabies."

"The wolves protect us from outsiders; they attacked me for protecting you. Their bite isn't dangerous. Don't run off again. I thought I'd have a heart attack when Kevin told me you'd gone into the forest." There was no anger in his voice, only concern.

"I didn't run off for the hell of it," she pointed out, wrapping the bandage around his arm and securing it with some tape. "Kevin was bringing in wood for the fire, and he left the door open. I was going after Jones; he would have frozen if I had left him out there all night."

"I could have helped you look."

She looked at Mason, realising how close they were. *How have I never noticed the light ring of blue in his eyes?*

"You were too busy being angry with me for cleaning your father's office," she said, realising that she was shivering from the shock now there was nothing to distract her.

"I'm sorry for lashing out at you; you were trying to do something nice. Dad had his own chaotic way of dealing with everything. Seeing everything so organised... He never would have done such a thing, and seeing it..." He paused, raking his hands through his hair. "Seeing it hurt more than I expected it to. I realised he would never come back to make it a mess again."

Emotion caught in her throat. She knew the exact feeling. It was why her mum's art studio was untouched in her house.

"It hurts to know they aren't coming back, but I think he would be honoured to pass on the space to you. It was what he wanted most – for you to take his place," she said, breathing into her numb hands. She tried to still her body, but the shaking was getting worse. She clutched her hands and glanced down at them. "I'm sorry about the ring. I'll look for it."

"It doesn't matter; what matters is that you're safe. We'll have to get you a new one," he said with a slow smile.

A new one? Why go to the trouble? She didn't want to lose another, but there were only so many days left.

"Peace?" she offered, extending her hand.

"Peace." He took her hand, running his thumb along hers. The pleasant sensation caused her to drop his hand.

He cleared his throat, scratching the back of his neck as an awkward tension filled the air between them.

"I should say thank you for organising the office. I'm sure Mum will be happy. She still has to work in there – I'm sure it will make her life easier. She couldn't have brought herself to do it." Concern creased Mason's brow as he watched her shake. "You need to take off your clothes."

She frowned at him. "Really? Now is not the time!"

He leaned forward with a smile, his hands on either side of her thighs, and she felt more nervous now than she had been staring at the horde of wolves.

"I'm flattered, but you'll freeze if you don't get out of those wet clothes," he said. "There should be some clothes in the bedroom. Though I don't know when anyone was here last."

Lyla looked at the table, eager to change the topic, and noticed an e-reader on it.

"Can't be that long ago," she said, picking it up. "I have a newer version of this." When she clicked it on there was still battery left, and a list of classics appeared. *Definitely not mine* – she thought of the endless romances and crime novels on hers. She handed it to Mason.

"I can't believe he was actually using it," he marvelled. "It was a present I got for my dad the last Christmas before I left. I didn't think he'd even open it. We used to come here before the season began." He cleared his throat, turned it off, and placed it on the table.

"Seems like he loved it," Lyla said.

"Not that he would have told me," he grumbled.

She got up, noticing the photos of a very young Mason on the mantle. She had never seen him smile so honestly before. "Cute kid – wonder what went so wrong," she joked.

Reaching over her shoulder, he flipped down the picture. "He grew up." He left for the bedroom, leaving her to examine the photos. She recognised one, recalling the sleigh and the younger Klaus family – it was the same family photo Mason had on his bedside table at home. When she had seen it before, she never would have guessed it had been taken in a secret village.

If I had never taken him home, if I hadn't left the party, none of this would have happened. I would be with Sam watching too many Christmas movies, not in a cabin with the one person in this world I swore never to like.

"There are some clothes on the bed for you," Mason told her when he came back, having changed into a new jumper and tracksuit bottoms. She found it hard to look away. The man in the suit she could hate, but seeing him like this did something to her insides she couldn't ignore.

She went to the bedroom and found a pair of leggings and a knitted jumper. Once she was changed, she joined him on the couch. There was a cup of hot tea waiting for her, and she quickly clasped it in her hands, needing all the heat she could get. It wasn't enough.

"Keep chattering like that and I'll throw you to the wolves," Mason mocked, looking up from the e-reader.

"I'm sorry my hypothermia is bothering you," she said, moving to the edge of the couch. She tried to pull the blanket onto herself, but Mason was sitting against it. "Can you lean forward? I feel like the cold is eating my bones."

He shifted, but she pulled the blanket too quickly, causing him to drop the e-reader. He picked it up and placed it on the table.

A tense silence gripped them, and then he surprised her by pulling her onto his lap, straddling him. She gasped at the contact and tried to wriggle away, but he held her tight.

"What are you doing?" she exclaimed. She considered moving way, but the warmth of his body forced her to settle against him, the contours of his body melding to hers.

"Body heat is the best way to warm up," he said, and she could hear the satisfaction in his voice. She tried to lean back to look at him, but he held her waist so she couldn't move.

"I think we have to be naked for that to work," she said breathlessly, her chest pressed tightly against his. He was so warm, and the way his body fitted into hers made her snuggle closer, craving every inch of him, even if her mind told her it was a bad idea.

"That can be arranged."

"I'm not in the mood to be played with," she warned, as his hands drifted from her waist to her thighs.

"Who says I'm playing? I'm merely thinking about your health," he teased, his breath against her neck.

With only the thin leggings separating his fingers from her skin, she resisted the compulsion to lean into his touch. She braced her hands on the back of the couch, sensation stirring between her legs as she felt him beneath her.

"I think I'm warm enough now," she breathed when his hands slipped beneath the edge of her sweater to brush her ribs. She shivered; his hands were like ice, but they caused her to burn.

"I don't think so. You're still shivering," he said, a smile on his lips.

"It's the shock," she lied, feeling his heartbeat quicken against her chest. *He isn't immune to me either.*

He took the blanket from beside them and wrapped it over her shoulders, shrouding them both as he leant back against the couch. She listened to the sound of his breathing, the beat of his heart. Slowly, the panic of what had happened in the forest began to subside.

"Thank you for stopping the wolves," she muttered, though it pained her to admit she needed his help. She was trying not to think about how she was wrapped around her extremely sexy and protective partner – her mortal enemy.

He didn't respond, only sat back a little, forcing her to look at him. His eyes settled on her lips, and her heart stilled as she realised she was longing for him to kiss her. She watched him swallow, and assumed he was thinking the same thing. His hands gripped her thighs, as if to pull her closer.

She closed her eyes, bringing her lips to his... but instead of meeting her halfway, his grip tightened and he lifted her off his lap, settling her beside him. A lump of mortification settled in her throat.

"You should stay in front of the fire. I'll take the bedroom," he said abruptly.

Lyla was too embarrassed to look at him, so she nodded and wrapped the blanket tighter around herself, missing the feel of him, the security of his body. Something had shifted inside her, and it pained her to admit what she felt, while he seemed unmoved.

"There's some boiled water in the kettle on the stove – don't drink from the tap." His voice held no emotion, only a warning. "The bathroom is through the kitchen," he finished, running his hand through his hair, and she noticed he was flushed.

Maybe he isn't as unaffected as I thought. She fought the urge to rise and kiss him, to admit to the tension between them and give in to the temptation that was sure to consume them both.

"And the wolves won't get in?" She couldn't bring herself to say anything else. Maybe if she admitted her fear he would stay with her on the couch. She couldn't help wondering how long the torches outside would last, considering how much snow was falling.

"The cabin is warded against them; the torches are added protection." His smirk was enough to remind her how much he irritated her. "Don't worry, you can sleep easy. I won't let the big bad wolves get to you."

Warded? "And who's going to protect me from *you*? This is the second time I've almost lost my life since I've arrived." She closed the gap between them, forcing him to look at her. Her heart was more in danger than her life, even if he couldn't see it.

"If you hadn't run away—" he argued, stepping closer, but she was too tired to go in circles, even if it was fun to watch the veins bulge in his neck as his temper flared.

"Goodnight, Mason." She turned her back on him, settling on the couch.

He said nothing, but he hesitated, and she wondered if she should turn around. Finally, she heard the creak of the warped floorboards telling her he had left the room, and then the door closing. Her fingers grazed her lips, remembering how much she'd been tempted to kiss him. The feel of his hands on her waist, and how she had arched into his embrace... She squeezed her eyes shut and pulled the blanket tighter.

The cold made you do it, she reassured herself, but an inner voice told her it had been much more than his body heat calling to her. Lyla forced herself to sleep before that same voice tempted her feet towards his bedroom door.

CHAPTER SIXTEEN

Sitting at the breakfast table, Lyla picked at a protein bar she'd found in the cupboard. Thankfully her jeans and jumper had dried overnight, so she was warm and fed – for the most part. It would have to do until they got back to the main house. Mason wasn't up yet.

Jones distracted her from her pathetic breakfast by pawing at the closet door.

"What are you looking for?" she asked, wondering if he smelt something. "Please don't let it be a mouse!" She opened the door cautiously to find that it was full of jackets, a shovel, bucket and a mop. Jones wandered in and, much to her surprise, knocked his head against the bucket, which contained two pairs of skates.

Crouching down to pick up the cat, she noticed Mason's name engraved on one pair. Back home, she remembered how he had turned his desk away from the ice rink.

Why did he say he hated skating? From the wear on these he must have done it a lot.

She gathered the evidence and shoved open the bedroom door to find Mason sleeping on his back, his blankets askew, revealing his broad chest. The sight of him stirred an ache in her she wasn't proud of. Focusing on his face, which wasn't much better, she climbed onto the other side of the bed and dumped the skates on him, not caring how heavy they were. He woke with a start, sitting up as the heavy boots winded him.

"You told me you couldn't skate," Lyla accused.

Mason looked like he was going to strangle her with the laces as he shoved them off.

"I told you I don't like skating. There's a difference," he groaned, rubbing his eyes. The blanket had fallen to his waist. Lyla noticed the freckles on his shoulders and had the sudden desire to count them – with her tongue. Thankfully, he rose and pulled on a jumper before she could complete such a mission.

He went to the bathroom without another word, and it only struck her then: maybe skating brought up some unpleasant memories. The man had more layers than a tiramisu, but she was determined to figure him out. She waited for him in the kitchen, leaving the skates outside the bathroom for him to discover, or trip over.

"This pair was my sister's. They should fit you," Mason said gruffly, dumping a smaller pair of skates on the table before going to the stove, where she had made coffee. He picked up the cup and smelt it before taking a sip. Lyla couldn't resist a little smile when he didn't contest it. In the office, his coffee order was never made right; he had almost driven the PAs to drink after their multiple failed attempts. Here, perfection didn't seem to matter as much to him.

"You're going to skate?" she asked excitedly, sitting at the table with her knees tucked under her chin in an attempt to keep warm.

Mason rolled his eyes, nodded, and finished the rest of the coffee before replying. "You survived a pack of wolves, so I can spare you five minutes on the ice – but then I have to get to the workshop."

"What am I going to do for the rest of the day? I'm not going back to the village to face your dearest Natalie after what happened at the gingerbread contest. I might have to curl up and die," she said.

He crouched in front of her. "I couldn't have you suffer another near-death experience, so I think there's something you need to see."

"What would that be? Elves?" she asked, nervous about what else he could possibly surprise her with.

"Elves don't exist. Sorry to disappoint you. But I can show you how it all works – separate the fact from the fiction. As a Christmas fanatic, I'm surprised you haven't done your own exploring."

"Not when there are wolves outside the door... and I didn't want to risk causing trouble," she admitted, though it went against everything in her nature not to snoop.

"I think you make enough trouble as is," he said, hiding a smile behind his mug.

"Think how dull your life would be without me," she replied, putting her knees down.

Mason avoided her gaze and went to the window, pulling back the sheer curtain. "The snow has stopped for now, and the ice should be thick enough."

"Then we should get moving before you turn back into the Grinch."

He glared at her while she secured the ice skates to her feet.

"I need more coffee if I'm going to do this," he muttered, taking her mug and drinking what was left. It was a small gesture, but the intimacy of his lips touching where hers had only made her jealous of the mug.

"Help yourself," she snarked, before he began securing his own boots.

"Stay away from the centre," Mason warned, skating out onto the frozen lake.

Lyla shook her head in amazement as she witnessed how at ease he was. She guessed it had been years since he'd last skated, and yet there was no hesitation in his movements. He came back towards her as she stepped off the snowy bank. The ice was rougher than she was used to, but she was determined not to struggle.

"It tends to be quite thin, and I don't plan on saving your life twice in two days," he warned, skating circles around her.

"Do you have to be the best at everything you do?" she muttered to herself.

"Do you want me to lead you?" he asked sincerely, and she slapped away his hands.

"I know how to skate!" she snapped, taking long strides, loving the sensation of the ice scraping beneath her blades. The joy of it made her lose focus, and when she was about to catch up to him, her boot clipped a rough piece of ice. She landed painfully on her knees, and her hands grazed the ice. To her horror, a crack sounded as she landed.

Mason, skating towards her, couldn't contain his laughter.

"How can you *laugh?* I heard a crack!" She couldn't

hide the terror in her voice. "You said *not* to skate in the centre."

"Don't worry, it won't crack. I wanted to see your reaction." He offered her a hand, which she gratefully took as the ice melted into her trousers. "The lake is frozen year-round," he added while she wiped her sore palms on her jeans. He offered his hands again, and she skated away a little, trying to hide the flush of embarrassment on her cheeks.

"I don't need you to lead me. I can skate fine." She attempted to shoot ahead, but a ridge in the ice caught her blade and she nearly went down for a second time.

"Rough ice isn't the same as a rink," Mason explained, taking her hand as he skated up beside her.

"The bruises on my knees are telling me the same." His fingers wove in between hers, and she let him guide her round the ice.

"If you told me a week ago that I'd be putting bruises on your knees, I wouldn't have believed it."

"Ha-ha. How easily you take joy in my misery."

He winked, picking up the pace, and she kept up, reassured by his grasp.

"I don't know why you left all this – this place, your family – to be alone in the city," she said. He stared out at the lake without responding, though his pace slowed a little. "Do you even enjoy being away?" she pressed. She had seen him smile more in the past few days than in the year they had worked together.

"It's easy not to appreciate what you have. You think this is everything, but I wanted to see the world, to see more," he admitted. *A vague answer.*

"What made you leave? Because, seeing you with your family, there had to be some kind of tipping point..."

Mason released her. She took advantage of the silence to

spin until she was too dizzy to continue. When she glanced at him again, the ease was gone from his eyes.

"Why do you want to know?" he asked, stopping in the middle of the lake.

"It's something you would tell your fiancée?" she joked, trying to lighten the mood.

"Then it's a good thing you aren't really my fiancée," he said, blowing into his hands.

"What's the point in being mysterious? I already know who you are – you're a freaking Klaus! A real-life Santa Claus, who grew up in a magical village! But you won't tell me why you left. I don't believe it was because you wanted to see the world."

He slid backwards, and she watched his skate catch on a pebble. Lyla reached out to catch him before he landed in the snow bank, but he was too heavy; instead, he took her with him. He held her tight in his arms as a puff of snow enveloped them and they landed in the pillowy snow.

"Serves you right for being so smug," she said, pressing her hand against his chest so she could get herself back upright.

"You distracted me with your prying," he argued.

"Fine. I won't pry any more. Until we're back on solid ground, anyway," she called over her shoulder, making her way back to the cabin and leaving him to follow.

CHAPTER SEVENTEEN

Argyle was waiting at the house to take them to the workshop; Mrs Klaus stood with him in her dressing gown and curlers, looking rather perplexed. Mason called out to her, and her shoulders relaxed.

"You've had your mother awfully worried," Argyle said when they reached the sleigh, and Lyla saw the glint of humour in his eyes.

"Where have you been? We've been worried sick!" Mrs Klaus reached for Lyla and turned her around, making sure she was okay.

"I'm okay, there's no need to worry," Lyla reassured her, and Mrs Klaus tutted.

"Running off into the forest! You could have been killed. Those pesky wolves could have gobbled you up."

"Don't worry, Mum, I got to her before she became dinner," Mason interjected.

"Kevin told me about the fight. You shouldn't have yelled at her – she did a great job on the office!" Mrs Klaus scolded him, slapping his arm.

He winced, and his mother's fretting turned to concern. She took her son's hand, rolling up the sleeve to reveal the bandage.

Lyla watched Mason let her examine the wound without any fuss or complaint. She figured Mrs Klaus wasn't a woman to say no to.

"You were scratched? Got to her in time – just in time to put yourself in danger." Mrs Klaus dropped his arm.

"Bitten, but Lyla cleaned me up in the cabin. We should really do it up. Some renovation and we could all go up together in the future," Mason said.

Mrs Klaus's eyes widened. "If you'd like to, we can. Lou hasn't visited it in years; I don't think Sara has even seen it. It's been a while since we were all up there," she said with a hopeful smile.

Lyla bit her lip, worrying that Mason was giving her false hope if he intended to leave after the season. She could see how much Mrs Klaus had missed her son, and she would be hurt enough when their fake engagement came to an end.

"I'm sorry, I shouldn't have run off. I couldn't let Jones go," she said, clutching him close to her chest.

"I would have probably done the same, but next time don't go off alone," Mrs Klaus said sympathetically as the cat popped his head out from Lyla's jacket. "Naughty boy, running off and causing trouble. Let's get you some food." Mrs Klaus took him from Lyla and cradled him in her arms. "I told Argyle you're taking Lyla to the workshop – about time she saw it," she added to Mason, leaving them with the sleigh.

"Come on, hop in. No point in arguing with her," Argyle said, opening the door for them.

Lyla wasn't sure how she felt about seeing the workshop. As much as she longed for answers, to know more about Mason and where he came from, she wondered if the truth would ruin the magic of Christmas. Was blissful ignorance better, so that when she returned to reality, her life would go on unaltered? *I could tell the council I've changed my mind and have them wipe my memory. Or, we play out our engagement and leave once the season ends, then I can keep my memories of this magical place.* She wasn't sure which was better, and she feared she wouldn't know until it was too late.

But there was no time for doubts; Mason shoved her into the sleigh, stating that they were going to be late, and he wanted to catch the foreman before he left.

They made the trip to the far end of the village in silence. Lyla needed some peace after all that had happened in the last twenty-four hours. She glanced at Mason, talking away to Argyle about finding her ring, and wondered if her feelings for him would continue back in the office. *Is it simply the magic of Yule pulling us together?*

The sleigh diverged onto a tree-crowded path and was met with a set of golden gates, which opened upon their arrival, just as the gates of Mason's home had on their first night. This time Lyla knew better than to wonder how. A warehouse made of logs greeted them. Lyla raised her hand as she noticed gold speckles drifting through the air and followed them to their source: a large chimney on the roof, pumping out the gold dust. She reached up to catch it. Gold coated her hand as the sleigh reached the doors to the workshop. She frowned at Mason when it disappeared from her skin.

"All answers will come in time," he said before she could ask.

She closed her mouth and followed him out of the sleigh. It was already starting to snow again, so she was grateful to go inside quickly, even if her stomach was in knots about what she would find.

"Good morning, Mr Klaus," a worker in red overalls said, holding the door for them. Lyla guessed he must be in his late sixties. He offered Lyla a polite smile, and she realised she was staring.

"Morning, Ian – how is the count going?" Mason asked. "The foreman," he added to Lyla in a whisper as Ian checked over the clipboard in his hand.

"Kevin dropped off the List this morning, so we should have enough Dust for everyone now that we have the final count," Ian told them.

Dust? List? Lyla tried not to appear as though she had no idea what he was talking about – and suddenly it clicked. She remembered how angry Mason had been when he'd discovered she had moved the list. Apparently without it, they couldn't work.

Of course they couldn't work. It's the freaking Naughty or Nice list! Her own conscience cursed her. She understood his anger better now, though she hoped never to see him so fierce again. They had already lost Mr Klaus; the thought of losing the list was sure to have furthered their pain immeasurably.

"Glad to hear we're back on track. Is Lou in?" Mason asked.

Ian shook his head. "She was here through the night, making sure the machines kept shuffling. Sent her back before dawn."

"So, nothing's changed," Mason said, and Ian laughed.

"Lou would work herself to death if we let her. Ten years without you, and I think she feels the responsibility of the season has fallen on her. But your father would be proud of you both working together now," the foreman said. Lyla guessed he had been close to the late Mr Klaus from his forlorn expression.

"I'll talk with her this evening then," Mason said, ignoring the rest of the statement. Lyla wondered when he would stop avoiding the mention of his father. He'd have to face it at some point.

"I'm sorry – we're being terribly rude," Ian said, offering Lyla a hand. She took it happily. "Not every day a newcomer brightens our door."

"Thank you for having me. I don't want to interrupt your work," she said, but Ian waved away the thought.

"Nonsense! We love to be disturbed. Gives us a chance for a break, and this close to the season, we could all use one."

"She's getting the full tour this morning. Thought it was time she learnt all our dirty little secrets." Mason pulled Lyla close, catching her by surprise. His mood swings were giving her whiplash. On the journey, he couldn't have sat further away, and now his hand was anchored at her waist.

"I heard talk of your fiancée; your uncle was positively fuming. Made my day seeing his pompous arse turn the same shade as the sleigh." Ian winked, and Lyla couldn't help but join in on the laughter. "Learning all the secrets of the season – careful. Once we let you in, we might not let you out!"

"Don't frighten her off! I would hate to have to chase her twice in twenty-four hours." Mason gave her a squeeze, and she pinched him in retaliation. The foreman gave them a confused look.

"It was nice to meet you – hopefully we'll meet again," Lyla offered, trying to change the subject.

"Enough of me taking up your time. Go on in out of the cold. There should be a fresh pot of coffee on, don't want you to freeze," Ian said, holding the door for them. Lyla was grateful to escape from the cold; she was trying not to let her teeth chatter.

"He seems like a good man," she said, once they were out of earshot.

"The best. He's worked for the family for years. I thought he would have retired by now, but he must have decided against it, given the circumstances," Mason explained.

"He seemed happy to see you."

"Nice try. I'm not telling you why I left."

"Why?"

"Why would I want to spoil a perfectly good day?" He turned her around to face the Workshop, and her words failed. "Welcome to where the magic happens."

A factory donned in a golden hue sat before her. The glow radiating from a giant glass hourglass sat at the centre of the room. Lyla was mesmerised by the flowing sand within, before realising it wasn't sand. She remembered the golden particles she'd been coated in outside. *This is the dust he was talking about.*

When she had thought of Santa's workshop she had always imagined elves and presents, but instead there were humans and gold dust. Lyla drifted away from Mason, who didn't stop her as she approached a wooden conveyor belt on which sat small red velvet pouches. She followed their path to the hourglass, where she watched workers opening the many golden taps attached to the base of the hourglass. The workers turned the tap, letting out a small amount of dust before tying the gold strings to seal each pouch.

"Those who collect the dust wear the green overalls," Mason said at her back. "The ones in red collect the pouches and add them to the sleighs for Christmas Eve."

He led her away from the hourglass to another set of doors, but before she could enter, he placed headphones over her ears.

"Are these necessary?" she shouted, unable to hear herself. He simply covered his own ears and opened the doors.

This room wasn't as magical. Half was exposed to the outside, letting in the snow, while machines carried in piles of fist-sized rocks and added them to a machine. The room was freezing, but she guessed the workers, constantly on the move, didn't feel it. The rocks were broken down with a fierce rattle, and what came out the other side was sifted until a black dust was formed. The workers all wore the same headphones and silver overalls. Lyla understood the reason for the ear protection now – she could hear the grinding and cracking of the stones even with the soundproofing, so she could imagine how loud it was without. With all the machines cranking and churning, and more flashing dials on the walls than she had seen in her entire life, it looked more like a manufacturing plant than anything else.

"Gold dust, black rocks – this is insane! I was expecting elves and toys," she called.

Mason only frowned, and they followed the conveyor belt back to where they had started.

"What did you say?" he asked once they could hear each other speak.

In front of the hourglass again, Lyla watched the black dust travel along the belt.

"I said this is insane! Rocks and gold dust instead of presents and elves," she said, reaching out to the dust.

The rocks had been crumbled to nothing before being fed through shifting layers repeatedly until the particles were so fine it was nearly impossible to pick up when she touched it.

"In this form, it's nothing," he said, letting the black dust run through his fingers. "It only transforms once it goes through the hourglass."

"When you said workshop, I thought there would be toys," she said as he brought her back to the hourglass.

"In a way, the dust is a present – but definitely not a toy."

Lyla stared at the black dust entering the top of the hourglass and drifting until it became glimmering golden particles.

"I can take you to see a few toymakers in the village if this doesn't live up to your expectations."

"Expectations? No one could expect this. It's so beautiful, but I have no idea what gold dust has to do with Christmas," she admitted.

They stood together, watching the changing dust.

"Every year, as we work, the hourglass fills with the dust. We mine the rocks from the Moiruilt Mountains which surround Yule. We don't know exactly how it works, but we know there's magic within them. Then, during the twelve days before Christmas, the taps open. The list decides who gets what."

"You don't decide?"

"No. The list writes itself. We create parchment from the trees here, and stack it in a room; as the year progresses, names appear. We check it, twice, to make sure it's correct."

"You check it? But if it writes itself, how could you possibly check it?"

"The list can change, from the beginning of the year to the end. We make sure we have the most updated version by making a copy of the original. At the end of the year, we have a team who checks it.

"The land decides to create the dust and the list. We are merely its workers and deliverers. On Christmas Eve, the list is placed in the hourglass. When the night is over and all the dust distributed, all that remains in the hourglass is the completed list; if everyone has received their dust, then the names on the list turn gold," he said reverently.

Lyla had more questions than answers, but maybe when dealing with such magical properties it was a matter of faith rather than fact. One thing did puzzle her. "I've never received gold dust at Christmas. I checked the list, and I was on the nice column!"

Mason picked up a velvet pouch from the conveyor belt and opened it. He took her hand in his and poured the gold dust over her open palm, only for it to evaporate.

Lyla ran her fingers over her palm, feeling... nothing. "I don't understand."

"No, you never saw the gold dust. The dust was sprinkled over you, your presents or something that belonged to you. It's like goodwill – a touch of luck so your year will be better than the last. A gift doesn't always have to be material. Myths of Klaus just found it easier to say we give presents rather than dust."

"And if you – if they're on the naughty list?" Lyla asked.

"Then they'll have to go without the helping hand until they decide to extend one to another."

Kind of like karma. "Clever," was all she could muster, watching the workers fill pouch after pouch until she grew dizzy. "So even those who don't believe receive something?"

"Just because someone doesn't believe in us doesn't mean we don't believe in them. This is why the village is so secret. This place is more than a workshop; we help keep the balance in the world. Without hope, kindness and generosity, the world would be a much darker place."

"You said we," she said.

"What?" he asked, his attention pulled from the hourglass.

"You said 'we'. I thought you had decided to leave this place behind."

"Don't twist my words," he said with a nudge.

"For all this talk of kindness and generosity, you became an investment banker?" she said under her breath, and then regretted it.

"Yes. I like money. In Yule, everything is faith; numbers are facts." He led her away from the factory floor, though she really wanted to stay and watch all day to make sure everything she was seeing was real.

"I also save businesses; I don't close them. You made me the enemy before I even said hello," he reasoned.

"You made yourself the enemy when you stepped into my seat without so much as a hello," she countered, but she knew how much he had helped her company, even if she didn't want to admit it.

He clenched his jaw, reminding her of their past tiffs; all he was missing was the suit. She followed him up a stairway to the second level of the open warehouse, where there was a small office. He closed the door once she was inside, giving them some peace from the ruckus below, then stood by the door, watching her.

"If you understand why Christmas is so important, why didn't you want to celebrate?" she asked, taking a seat at his desk.

He shrugged, avoiding the question.

"I suppose after having so many Christmases here, celebrating it out in the real world wouldn't be as fun." She leant back in the chair as he walked to the other side of the desk.

"Comfortable?" he asked, raising his eyebrows as she rocked back and forth.

"It does feel good to take your seat for a change." She grinned, and he concealed his own by rubbing his jaw.

"You can sit at my desk *any* time."

She rolled her eyes. "Flirting with me to avoid my questions – that's a new tactic. Though I think I prefer it to being scolded," she said, resting her elbows on the desk. *If he wants to play the flirting game, so be it.*

He walked around the desk and turned the chair so she was facing him. "If it's what you prefer, I'd be more than happy to oblige," he drawled, placing his hands on the armrests on either side of her.

She leaned forwards, daring him to meet her halfway.

"Since when are you so generous?" she teased, staring at his lips, so close to her own.

He moved closer. "Fight with you, flirt with you – I'll do whatever you want if it keeps you close."

His bold words surprised her. He reached for her, tilting her chin up so she was forced to meet his mischievous gaze. She searched it for answers. *Does he truly want me? Or is this a game?* Her breath caught as he traced a thumb over her cheek, before slipping his hand beneath her curls to the back of her neck.

She remembered the last time he had dared to flirt. He had been drunk; this time he was stone-cold sober. He had barely touched her, but the thought of more made her breath quicken.

There was a knock on the door, and Mason straightened up as a woman with thick-rimmed glasses walked in holding a box of presents.

"Mace, your mum asked me to drop these off for the gala raffle. Could you make sure she gets...?" The woman looked between them. Lyla pushed out of the chair and away from Mason. They hadn't been doing anything, but they didn't look innocent either.

Even if she thought they were up to something, the older woman didn't give anything away. She put the box down on the couch before extending her arms towards Lyla and embracing her tightly. "This must be Lyla! I've heard all about you. I didn't think we would get a chance to meet before the gala!"

The hug was tight enough to cut off her air supply, but Lyla didn't mind.

"Don't suffocate the poor woman," Mason said, already looking through the wrapped presents. "Anything worth bidding on this year?"

"Plenty," she scowled, slapping his hands away. Lyla took a relieved breath. The contagious happiness in Yule could be a little overwhelming, but she couldn't help liking it. "I'm June – I run a bakery in the village. You should stop by. I can make you anything you like," she beamed.

Lyla could never say no to a pastry; she had the curves to prove it.

"I can never turn down coffee and cake," she said eagerly, returning the woman's smile. She guessed June must be as old as or older than Mrs Klaus. That she had managed to carry the heavy box of presents up the flight of stairs was impressive.

"I'll dash, but we'll see you at the lights festival tonight, and the gala in a few days? It's tradition – to mark the beginning of the end to the season with a grand celebration. Mason's return has brightened up the village," June said in a flurry.

Lyla didn't know what to say. "I'm sure I'll talk to you then," she offered.

June looked at Mason, who was still poking through the box. Lyla got the impression he'd been one of those kids who liked to peek at his presents before Christmas Day.

"Your arrival gave us all something to focus on," June whispered. "Oh, goodness – you arrived so late! What are you wearing for the gala? You'll need to be fast before the dresses are all gone. With only a few days to go, it's too late to book the dressmaker now, but I'm sure we can find you something." She clasped her hands under her chin.

Lyla felt the pressure of the lies she'd told start to crawl up the back of her neck, bringing with it an instant headache. She was meeting so many people; knowing how much her arrival meant to them only made her feel worse. She thought of their failed dress shopping and wished she had bought the red dress.

"Don't worry too much. I have everything under control," Mason said, joining them. Lyla wondered if that was another one of his lies.

"Glad to hear it!" June said.

"It wouldn't be a party without my fiancée," he added, and she forced a smile as he kissed the side of her head.

"Then we'll see you there. Make sure to bring your dancing shoes!" June grinned, disappearing out the door.

"You need to stop telling people we're getting married. Constantly reminding them we're engaged only builds on the lies," Lyla said. She hated the thought of such happy people being disappointed when she disappeared back home.

"Worried they might miss you?" Mason asked, releasing her.

"No, I'm worried someone will pry and find out we

aren't engaged," she argued, putting some distance between them. Being so close to him only muddled her thoughts.

"Only a few more days, and then you can leave and be forgotten."

"Nice to know I'm so easy to forget," she muttered. "But how are you going to explain my absence?"

"I'll tell them you couldn't face leaving your world behind. Others have left for the same reason. The council won't wipe your memory, if you leave honestly."

"So they would only wipe my memory if they discovered our deception?"

"Yes – they aren't barbarians. All outsiders are given a choice to stay or leave. However, if they think you've betrayed their trust, they wouldn't trust you with keeping Yule's secrets."

"This is making my head hurt."

"I don't make the rules. Unless this is your way of confessing your love for me and telling me you want to stay and turn our lie into a truth?" He was blocking her path to the door.

Lyla's eyes flashed to his, and there was a tense silence. She saw the uncertainty in Mason's eyes, and it made her heart hammer in her throat.

Crossing her arms, she stepped closer.

"Never."

CHAPTER EIGHTEEN

"There you both are! We're going to the festival to watch the lights!" Mrs Klaus said as Lyla and Mason walked into the house. Kevin and Lou were by her side, dressed to go out for the evening.

After spending the day learning about the ins and out of the workshop, Mason and Lyla had gone for dinner, then to an ice cream shop that served the best peppermint ice cream Lyla had ever tasted. They'd reached home tired and full. All Lyla could think about was a hot shower and bed. Her nose was so cold after a day of walking she thought it might snap off.

"Lights? June mentioned it was tonight," Mason groaned.

Lyla looked at him questioningly, and suddenly realised he was holding her hand. She didn't know when he had taken hold of it.

"Fireworks. There's a display to mark the sixth day before Christmas at midnight," he explained.

"And there are crafts and food stalls, a few games," Lou said, coming out of the sitting room.

"I think Lyla's tired," Mason told them. "We've had a long day. You can go on without us."

"Sorry – family rules. You can't get out of the lights festival," Lou said playfully.

Lyla didn't want to go against his eldest sister, so she squeezed Mason's hand, telling him it was okay to attend. As Mason continued to argue with his sister anyway, Kevin crept up beside them. Gone were his usual band T-shirts; in their place he wore a pale blue shirt that brought out his eyes. Lyla noticed they were lighter than Mason's.

"Ian came by the house, said you went to the workshop. There's no leaving us now that you know all our secrets," he said with a grin.

Before she could stop it, nervous laughter erupted from her. She certainly didn't want to continue a conversation about secrets, so she interrupted the arguing siblings.

"I would love to go. Grandpa here can stay and have a nap," she announced, elbowing Mason in the side. Her shower would have to wait.

"Then it's settled. We're all going," Lou said.

Bells rang through the village. When they turned into the village square, Mason stopped, and Lyla saw a mass of villagers holding candles and singing around the Christmas tree.

"Is this a vigil for your father?" Lyla asked.

"Unless you know of anyone else who died," he said,

and tried to turn them down an alley while his family went ahead, lost in their own conversations, and then into the gathering crowd.

"Shouldn't you stay?" Lyla said, taking his arm.

He resisted her pull towards the crowd like a petulant child. "Why? I know he's gone; do I need to spend the night dwelling on it?"

"I thought there was a light festival?" she coaxed.

"There is, but lord knows how long this is going to go on before the displays begin," he muttered, pulling up the collar on his jacket as people in the crowd started to stare at them. "If we don't stay, I can take you to have the best gingerbread you've ever had. It'll ruin you for any other for the rest of your life," he whispered.

"As tempting as baked goods are, I'm sure your family would want you to stand with them. For you to have some closure," she reasoned, slowly guiding him towards the crowd. He didn't fight her this time, merely gave in with a sigh.

The villagers were quick to let them through so they could stand with the others. Mrs Klaus gave them a sympathetic look, standing before the decorated tree that towered above the village. Mason placed an arm around his brother and whispered something that made Kevin chuckle. Lyla let him go, knowing he wasn't going anywhere.

"Who said you could let go?" Mason whispered, taking her hand in his.

She gripped his hand tighter for reassurance as she noticed the tears in his eyes.

One by one, people in the crowd recounted their memories about the late Henry Klaus. Ian stood on the candlelit podium, a sad smile creasing his features as he spoke.

"Henry was the only man I knew who could sleep standing up. There was more than one occasion when we would be talking away, then my words would go unanswered, and he would be standing there, List in hand, eyes closed. Maybe I bored him into slumber – but more likely he'd spent the week in the workshop and neglected to sleep, to eat. If it wasn't for our own Mrs Klaus, Henry probably would have forgotten to take care of himself. He was brutally honest, and never minced his words, but he believed in us, in our yearly mission. He believed that bringing some luck, some magic to the world was more important than any of us. He put his heart and soul into Yule, and though he would hate us all doting on his memory, he'd never have turned down an opportunity to gather everyone together for a celebration."

Lyla wondered if the Klaus family would speak, but they remained in the crowd, listening with sad smiles and laughs as jokes were told and stories of past Christmases were looked back on. Mason's grip grew tighter until finally the vigil ended with a series of glorious fireworks lighting up the sky, and even then, he didn't let her go.

"Hot whiskey?" Lou offered, balancing the tray on her lap.

Lyla took it and placed it on the table. The pub was crowded and stifling, but the laughter and music were comforting. There was no talk of business or contracts, only old stories and idle chit-chat that no one would remember tomorrow thanks to the generous measures of alcohol.

"I don't think she should have another," Mason said, nudging Lyla, who already had a warm glow in her cheeks after one too many eggnogs.

"I'd *love* one," Lyla said, silencing Mason with a finger to his lips.

"It's your hangover. The eggnog is lethal by itself," he warned.

Kevin called him to play darts, and he got up. Lyla was pleased to see them talking.

"I think you brought back a clone of my brother. I never thought he would come to the vigil," Lou commented.

"I was thinking the same thing! I'm glad you didn't listen to me about the letter," Sara said, sitting between Lou and Lyla.

She was in silver overalls, and her cropped hair was clipped away from her petite features. Lyla had been delighted to finally be able to put a face to the name when Lou had introduced them on the way to the pub.

"You didn't want her to send the letter?" Lyla asked, remembering first-hand what had happened as a result.

Sara explained before Lou could interrupt, "I wanted her to contact him earlier – it had been so long. I knew it hurt her when he couldn't come to our wedding." Lyla looked to Lou and saw her disappointment at the memory. "Mrs Klaus thought it might cause a scene if he came." Sara winced. It was disheartening to know that Mason had missed out on his sister's wedding because of the fight with his father, and that Mrs Klaus had been the one to suggest he keep away.

"That sounds awful – it was more that Mum didn't want our day to become another battlefield. I did reach out, and Mason still sent a present and a card, but then it was back to nothing," Lou chimed in.

"I wish we had invited him; they could have put the fight behind them."

"Mason wouldn't have come unless it was Dad who wrote, and he was too stubborn to be the first to reach out," Lou said, and everyone at the table fell into a short silence.

"He's here now, and that's what matters," Sara said at last, and Lou looked at her brothers.

"I only hope he wants to be – we need him. Not just for the season; I don't want him to disappear again. I think it would hurt Kevin too."

"I don't think that will happen," Lyla found herself saying, even if she knew that she would be the one to disappear. "He wanted to be here – he just needed permission to be."

Lou lifted her glass to her, and Lyla took a healthy gulp, comforted by the rush of warmth in her veins.

"Do *you* know his decision?" Lou asked.

"To become a Klaus? I don't know – he won't talk about it. Am I getting the title wrong? The title is Klaus, right? Not Santa Claus?" she asked, full of alcohol confidence. She was so used to calling Mason 'Klaus' that it was strange to think she had unknowingly been calling him by his formal title. *Maybe calling him Klaus only furthered the hostility between us? I was inadvertently reminding him of home.*

"Santa Claus is one of the names, but here in Yule, it's Klaus."

"I hope he does take the seat. That way the pressure will be lessened for you," Sara said, looking to Lou.

Lyla was surprised by her openness. "Pressure? Do the council want you to take the seat?" she asked Lou, who sighed.

"Oh, they tried to convince me. But it would take me away from the sleighs and away from Sara. Working together means we get to spend the days together. I'm where I can do the most," Lou said, taking Sara's hand. Sara blushed, and Lyla could see how much they loved each other. She wondered how anyone could put up with such pressure. She was relieved she had never known what it felt like to have a life forced upon her.

"You mentioned before you liked to race sleighs; is that how you got hurt?" she asked, looking at Lou's legs, covered by a thick blanket. "Sorry, I shouldn't ask – the eggnog has got to my curiosity."

"I don't mind. I thought Mum would have told you. No, I've never crashed racing. It was a stupid accident. I was tightening the bolts beneath Dad's sleigh, and the sleigh lift, what we use for working on the undercarriage, gave out. I haven't been out of the chair since." Lyla saw Sara's pained expression, though she didn't show it to Lou. Instead, she took a drink.

Lyla took another sip. "There was nothing they could do?"

"No, but I can still do most things I love. I've learnt to accept it, mostly. There's always going to be a part of me that never will." Lou sighed, but the conversation was interrupted by a group at the bar calling out to her and Sara. Any sorrow in her eyes was gone in an instant, and the smiling Lou was back.

"They must have finished repairing the engines," Sara said, getting up from her chair.

"One vital question I *have* to know," Lyla said in mock seriousness.

"You have our full attention," Lou said, and Sara leant in.

"Do the sleighs really fly?"

Lou and Sara laughed. "How else can we deliver gifts? But the ones we use around the village don't."

Lyla couldn't believe it. "What makes the delivery sleighs special?"

"Excellent engineering on our part – and a touch of magic," Lou said, and Lyla, perhaps thanks to the influence of one too many eggnogs, believed her wholeheartedly. She wanted to ask more questions, but Sara waved to the group across the bar.

"Our friends are here; do you want to join us? I'm sure they would love to meet you," Lou said, grabbing their drinks as Sara took the brakes off her chair.

"No, you two go ahead. I think I'll get some air. It was lovely to finally meet you, Sara," Lyla said. So much had come at her in the last few days, she needed a moment to breathe.

Sara beamed. "Me too. I can't wait for you to join the family."

Outside, the full weight of what she had drunk hit her. With a wobble, she sat on the bench outside the pub and put her head between her knees to stop the fairy lights outside the pub spinning.

"Let's get you home," Mason said, appearing beside the bench. She wasn't sure how long she had been outside before he appeared.

"I don't need your help," she slurred. *I did not realise how much that last drink had gone to my head.* "How did you know I was out here?"

"Yes, you do, and I knew because Lou said you went outside for some air. Don't worry, the eggnog kills us all the first time. By tomorrow, you'll be one of us," he said, helping her stand. She leaned against him.

"You smell like... nutmeg," she said, burying her nose in his jumper as she tried to feel her feet.

"And you smell like whiskey," he replied.

"I only had three! And some eggnog, but that can't count," she argued.

"That would be about six drinks here. Our measures are quite large," he laughed, to her horror. She *had* thought the drinks tasted a little stronger than she'd expected...

"The world really needs to stop spinning," she pleaded as they made their way to the end of the alley. "Just give me a second. I'm not drunk, only a bit dizzy." She relaxed against the archway.

"That's what happens when you have Lou's special eggnog," Mason said, breathing into his hands to warm them.

"What's special about it?"

"It's more brandy than it is eggnog." He smirked.

Lyla tipped her head back and tried to take a few deep breaths. Her eyes caught the mistletoe hanging from the archway, and she didn't know if it was impulse or the egg-nog, but she rose on her tiptoes and kissed him. Barely, but it was enough to make his eyes go wide.

She settled back against the archway with a smug smile.

"Sorry – it's the rules, and I think here of all places they must be followed," she told him.

He started to pace in front of her, clearly unsettled. "You've been drinking – we shouldn't," he said firmly.

She gripped his arms, mostly to stop him pacing. It wasn't helping her head.

"Am I supposed to wait until we're both grey and old?" she demanded, suddenly feeling as sober as a sinner.

He stared at her, then shook his head. His arms wrapped around her, supporting her as his lips met hers. Gentle and coaxing, he tasted like brandy and peppermint, and she never wanted to taste anything else.

He pressed her against the archway, the damp stone soaking through her clothes. The cold caused her to gasp, parting her lips, and his tongue tasted hers. She deepened the kiss until she wasn't sure where he began, and she ended.

Footsteps forced them apart. Breathless and embar-rassed, Lyla rested her forehead against his chest, trying to catch her breath. Every inch of her being was desperate for more. Once the passers-by were gone, Mason kissed her forehead.

"Let's get you home," he said softly, holding her close as he guided her up the path.

CHAPTER NINETEEN

They walked back to the house in silence. Lyla couldn't stop looking at her hand clasped in Mason's; the eggnog and his presence kept her more than warm enough for the walk home.

The walk also did an excellent job at sobering her. When they reached the house all she wanted to do was pull him inside and continue what they had started under the mistletoe, but he gently released her hand.

"I have to check on the reindeer for the night. Kevin forgot earlier because of the vigil," he said abruptly. She sensed he knew exactly what would happen if they went inside together.

"Right, duty calls," Lyla said, trying not to sound disappointed as he unlocked the door for her. "Don't be out too long – you still have to be up early tomorrow." She grimaced. She didn't know for a fact he needed to be up early; she had merely wanted to say something to cut through the tension.

She watched him head off to the barn, pulling up his collar against the cold, and felt the overwhelming urge to comfort him, to hold him and never let go. Instead, she went inside and closed the door behind her, because that was the sensible thing to do. Their situation was complicated enough; the last thing they needed was emotion messing everything up when she was only days away from leaving. She didn't know whether he was returning or not, and she was becoming unsure of what him staying meant to her.

After showering, she tried to sleep for around an hour, but it wouldn't come, so she opted to head downstairs and watch TV. She didn't know if it was the eggnog or the memory of Mason's lips keeping her awake.

The lights in the house had dimmed for the night and she tiptoed into the sitting room, but instead of looking for the remote control she found herself walking down the hallway towards the spare room Mason was using. He should be back by now, though he hadn't come to her room to check on her, so he must have decided to stay away for the night. She wondered if he was trying to be considerate of their arrangement, but she would have much rather he'd joined her.

Down the hall, she tapped on the door, to no answer. She knocked again, a little louder, but when there was still no answer she couldn't risk trying again in case someone heard and realised they weren't sharing a room.

Mrs Klaus had gone to bed hours ago, exhausted after the vigil. Lou would be with Sara, but she had no idea where Kevin was. Her hand hesitated on the doorknob. *Turn around and go back to the sitting room,* she warned herself, but she opened the door – to find a dark room and an empty bed.

He can't still be with the reindeer. Could he have gone back to the village or to the workshop? She took a breath. *Is he trying to avoid me because I kissed him? We agreed to this false relationship, but if there's something more between us, why is he running?* She closed the door softly behind her.

A loud thud down the hall stopped her on the way back to the kitchen. Following the sound of moving furniture and a series of loud curses, she reached Mr and Mrs Klaus's study. The door was ajar.

"Mason?" she called, knocking softly.

"Letters? Fucking letters," she heard Mason mutter from where he was sitting at his father's desk. A pile of envelopes lay on the desk before him. Drawers were open everywhere, and a cabinet had been shifted out of the way.

"What's going on?" Lyla asked.

He shoved the letters towards her. A few fell to the floor as he relaxed into the back of the chair. She picked up one and saw his name and address written on a red envelope in the same gold calligraphy that had brought them here.

"Your father wrote to you every year, but never sent them?" she asked. He nodded, and she checked the stamped dates on the envelopes of the unopened letters.

"Are you sure you never received any?" she dared to ask, and his dark eyes turned on her in warning.

"He never wrote," he affirmed grimly, his lips fixed in a firm line.

"Maybe he sent others that you didn't get? This place isn't exactly standard mail order," she reasoned, but that only seemed to further his annoyance.

"There are plenty of ways he could have sent them and if he had, I would have responded," he said, getting to his feet. She sensed he wanted some distance from the letters staring up at him. By the fire, he paced back and forth until she couldn't take it. She hugged him from behind, trying to offer him some comfort.

"Lyla?" he merely said, his hands going over hers.

"You're making me dizzy with the pacing," she joked, trying to ease the tension.

He sighed, dropping his head. She guessed it was what was within the envelopes that frustrated him so much.

"What do you want there to be in the letters?" she asked quietly. When he didn't reply, she moved around him so she could see his face.

"An apology... forgiveness," he said, staring down at her, before pulling her in close. Her cheek rested against his chest, and she let him continue without interruption. "I left because he forced me out," he admitted.

She pulled back in shock. "He forced you to go?" She couldn't believe it – his family were so loving, so kind. She couldn't imagine such a scene. Then again, Ian had mentioned that Mr Klaus had never minced his words.

"You asked me why I left. Growing up, all Dad cared for was the season, for the village, for making sure everything was perfect. Which is noble – he loved everything and everyone like they were his own – but the only way to get his attention was to *be* perfect. I did everything he asked of me, but when I finished school, I wanted to travel, to study away from home. In my naivety, I thought my father would be proud of me for wanting to make a name for myself."

"But he wanted you to stay?" she pressed, afraid he would close down again.

"I never planned on staying away, but the night I graduated, I told him I wouldn't marry Natalie as he wanted or go to work in the workshop full-time. I wanted to travel for a few years, and then I planned to come back and take up my share of the family responsibilities. He told me I had two choices: leave and never come back, or stay and take over."

"And you left."

"He didn't give me a choice. I knew that if I left, he would despise me. But if I had stayed and got married, I would have resented him. The marriage was just another way of ensuring I stayed here." He paused, starting to pace. "For years, he ignored me. Mum emailed when she could. Lou wrote from time to time – but from him, not a word in ten years. I couldn't even go to Lou's wedding because I knew we would fight. I didn't get to see Kevin grow up. The night of the party, I thought, finally, he's reaching out. He's getting older; he'll need me to return."

Lyla saw the tears in his eyes. After hearing all the kind words from the villagers, she could hardly believe his father would give him such an ultimatum. But she also knew that when a person died, their faults were forgotten, their sins forgiven, and all that remained was their good deeds.

She tried to close the distance between them, but he turned his back on her, picked up an armful of letters, and made to toss them into the fire. Luckily, she was faster than him. She lunged, placing her hands over his, ready to face his wrath rather than let him have another regret.

"Let go," he snapped. "This is none of your business."

She held firm. "You made it my business the minute you brought me here. I understand that he gave you an impossible choice, and for years you wondered what he was thinking, what he would say if he spoke to you. These will give you answers, even if his words are angry or pleading. You'll know what he was thinking, what he wanted to say, and you can't lose that," she insisted.

Mason's jaw tightened, but she didn't give in. She waited. At last his resolve wavered, easing his grasp on the letters, letting her take them. Lyla put them back in the desk drawer, hoping that if they were out of sight, they might be out of mind.

"Please let me be. Go back to bed. I want to be alone," he said, wiping tears away with his palms, but she refused to leave him. He sat on the floor, defeated by his grief.

"The last thing you need to be is alone," she told him. "You've spent too long alone." She knelt beside him on the rug before the fire. It had taken him days to break down, and it was only through his anger that the grief had found a way to surface.

She leaned in close, and he studied her, seeming unsure of what she was about to do. Lyla, determined to comfort him, kissed one cheek right where a tear had fallen, and then the other. She heard Mason's sigh of relief as he pulled her against him so that she had to wrap her legs around his waist.

"Bet you never thought you'd see this day, me breaking down in front of you," he mumbled, and she lifted his chin, forcing him to look at her. There was barely an inch separating them, and she listened to his breathing for a moment, felt the rising and falling of his chest level out.

"You lost someone you loved. You had no chance to say goodbye, and you only just learned he was trying to reconnect with you. Even if he wasn't successful, he wanted to. If you weren't breaking down, then I wouldn't be with you right now." She put her hand over his heart. "This is the Mason I want to know – to be close to. There's no shame in tears," she said.

His smile surprised her.

"It's only you I would allow get so close," he admitted, daring to kiss her ever so gently.

A test, and as soon as his lips brushed hers, she passed with flying colours, returning his kiss. This time there was no urgency, only longing. Emotions were high, and she didn't want to push him.

His tongue slipped between her lips, and she could taste the brandy on his tongue, spicy and sweet. Lyla's fingernails dug into his shoulders as she gripped him tightly, wanting, *needing* more of him as his lips trailed from her mouth to her neck. He nipped at her sensitive skin until she was grinding against him, desperate to satisfy the ache between her legs.

"You're so responsive," he murmured against her neck, trying to hold her hips still, but his hands slipped under her shirt, causing her to shudder. "You have no idea how much I want you, to worship your body until you don't remember anything but my name."

The only things separating them were her underwear and his jeans. Frustrated, Lyla reached down to feel him, and he groaned against her neck. She felt almost blinded by lust, and the heat of the fire was stifling. It was all too much, and she suddenly remembered why they were in the room in the first place. When she tensed he stopped his caresses, as if he'd had the same thought.

"Wait," she breathed, and he loosened his grip on her. When their eyes met, she saw the raw emotion in his eyes. "As much as I want you, we can't – not tonight," she told him, even if the persistent ache between her legs begged her to continue. She silenced her desire and eased back, giving them both some breathing room.

"We should stop," he agreed breathlessly. "I don't want you to think I'm only doing this because I'm—" He struggled to find the words.

Upset, grieving, angry, if not somewhat lost. With his

hands cupping her face, Lyla rested her forehead against his.

"Probably for the best," she admitted, but she wasn't going to let him spend the night alone in his grief. Since he wasn't releasing his hold on her, she figured he didn't want to be alone either. She got up.

"Come with me," she said, lifting his hand to her lips. She tried to lead him from the room, but he didn't budge.

"Where are we going? I'm in no mood to run from wolves," he joked.

"Was that a joke?" she demanded, and he offered her a crooked smile. "Come on, I'm not going to bite."

She pulled him again, and this time he followed her out of the office without protest. Once they reached her bedroom, Lyla climbed under the covers, and Mason hesitated before removing his jumper. With no T-shirt beneath, the sight of him did nothing to ease the warm sensation in her belly, but she forced herself to ignore it.

Without a word, he climbed in after her. His body cocooned hers and she snuggled closer, losing herself in him.

Chapter Twenty

Mrs Klaus found Lyla making breakfast for the family – or attempting to. She'd opted for fruit, without the strawberries, and pancakes. She didn't think she could mess it up too badly, and she'd been up early enough to hide the burnt and yet somehow undercooked attempts in the bin. Now they were golden, fluffy, and delicious.

"Morning, love. I wanted to let you know I have an email from a Samuel, in case you want to reply sooner rather than later. I didn't click in, don't worry," she said, and Lyla didn't doubt her.

The email. She had forgotten about the email and the share transfer.

"Are you alright? You've gone frightfully pale!" Mrs Klaus took the spatula from her hand.

"Just the aftereffects of Lou's eggnog," said Lyla.

"Thank you for telling me. I'd forgotten all about it." She took her apron off and headed for the office.

The laptop was already on and waiting for her. Sam had followed her instructions, and the email was pleasant, wishing her a happy Christmas. However, when she clicked on the attached file, she found Sam's real message, along with the document she'd asked for.

> Lyla, dearest!
>
> Where the hell are you?! I called and called. I was about to call the police when I got your email. New year and new CEO – what are you scheming at? A new year without the grouch is enough to make me cheer on your espionage.
>
> Attached are the documents you requested. Wherever you are, I hope you return a free woman.
>
> Looking forward to working for the new CEO. Also, Jamie says he is devastated you couldn't join us for a vegan Christmas dinner. He really wanted you to taste his watermelon turkey. However, corporate espionage must come first.
>
> Happy scheming, or Christmas!
> Your humble servant...

Lyla's stomach sank as she read the private message again. She cursed herself for being so impulsive and asking for the documents. She couldn't believe she'd thought she could use Mason's grief and his family to get him to stay here and give her the company.

But how are we supposed to work together now after everything that's happened? Could we run the company and be a couple? Our disagreements would kill us. We wouldn't last as partners, let alone a couple. She didn't want to regret the night before. She wanted to go back to bed and pretend she had never opened the email which had shocked her back to reality.

Company or not, whether he wants to stay in Yule or Dublin, I won't force him. She deleted the email without a second thought. Once it was gone, she went to trash and emptied it, leaving no trace behind. She couldn't bring herself to turn on him, not when he had shared so much. *His future is up to him, and I'm not going to threaten him with his identity.*

As relieved as she was to end her scheming, she was even more relieved not to taste a watermelon turkey. Not having to suffer that would be worth handing over her shares in total.

"Lyla?" Mason called, popping his head into the office. She jumped and slammed the laptop shut, and his frown spoke of his suspicion.

"Sorry – just a message from Dad. I didn't want him to worry in case he tried to reach me." She hated the lies falling so easily from her lips. But she couldn't tell him the truth, not now, not when she could lose him.

"How is he enjoying his Christmas? I'm sure his new wife is keeping him busy," Mason said, and there was a lightness to his expression which eased her worry for him. Last night had broken down his walls and let him feel the pain without it consuming him.

"Enjoying the sun," she said hurriedly, pushing aside the laptop as though it would burn her fingers. She went to him, and he hesitated before kissing her, which only made her smile. Whatever they were, whatever they were doing, it was obvious they both wanted it to continue.

"Breakfast is ready," he said, leading her down the hall.

"Smells great," she said, and he paused. "What?" she asked, sensing there was something else.

"For the gala tonight... Lou asked if you wouldn't mind doing her hair and make-up. Trust me when I say it's a cold day in hell when she asks for help."

"I'd love to help her!" Lyla was happy that Lou had some faith in her, and it would be nice to spend some time with her. Lou worked so hard; she deserved to get dolled up. "But I don't have a dress! We can't find one now; I can stay home. I think it would be better to put some distance between me and the villagers," she added quietly.

"There's no reason for distance. I want to show off my fiancée. As for the dress—" He kissed the side of her head. "I have everything under control."

She couldn't help the anxiety swelling in her chest. Even if their relationship couldn't be considered entirely untruthful, she worried they were walking on ice that was sure to break.

"I'm not wearing the bowtie," Kevin announced, interrupting her thoughts, when they reached the breakfast table.

"Yes, you will. It's customary. I'll be wearing one," Mason said, sitting beside his brother.

"Kevin doesn't mind wearing a bowtie, but he's refusing to wear the one you got him," Lou said to Lyla with a smirk, filling her bowl with porridge and fruit.

"Why? The gingerbread print is adorable!" Lyla and Mason had picked it out together as a joke when they went shopping. She didn't actually expect him to wear it, or for Mason to force him to.

"He thinks the person he likes won't like it," Lou said slyly.

Kevin threw a croissant at his sister, which resulted in a glare from Mrs Klaus.

"I made this food for you to eat, not throw. Wear the bowtie or don't – it's not a matter to get worked up over," his mum stated as Lou took a generous bite out of the croissant.

"You don't have to wear it," Lyla agreed, placing a hand over Mason's, not wanting him to fight with his brother.

"It was a gift, and it's a time-honoured tradition that if you receive a gift it must be worn, used or consumed," Mason said.

"Fine. If you feel so strongly about it," Lyla said, winking at Kevin, "then you wear it."

Mason rolled his eyes and Kevin thanked her by wrapping his arms around her. "I think you're becoming my favourite sister."

"I'm right here," Lou said, glaring at her brother.

"Can we please eat our breakfast in peace? It's going to be a long day," Mrs Klaus reminded them. Once Kevin went back to his seat, they did exactly that.

Mrs Klaus' hair was setting in curlers; she wrestled with some false lashes while Lyla finished Lou's make-up. She hadn't thought she would be able to attend the gala, but Lou had brought some of Sara's dresses and thankfully, there was one that fitted.

"Please thank Sara for me," she said to Lou, nodding to the black dress.

"Don't think on it – she was sad she couldn't get ready with us. She's with her family for dinner, but she'll join us there," Lou said. Lyla was glad she would know another person at the gala.

"If you let the glue set a little before you try to stick

them they should stay in place," she advised, as Mrs Klaus sighed at another failed attempt.

"I'm fairly sure my eyelashes are more glue than hair at this point." She threw down the false ones. "I give up – mascara will have to do."

Lyla picked up the mascara from the dressing table beside her and passed it over. "I think you're about done," she said to Lou.

Lou looked in the dresser mirror, examining her smoky eyes and dark red lips. With her pale blonde hair, she looked every bit the bombshell.

"I think you missed your calling," she said, squinting to get a better look at the winged liner.

"My mother was an artist; she could do wonders with a brush. This is as far as my artistic gifts extend," Lyla told her, closing the lid on the eyeshadow palette.

"She must have been very talented," Mrs Klaus said.

"She was incredible. She turned our townhouse into an art studio. Her work always sold out as soon as it was viewed. She brought nature to life – that's what she painted, landscapes, but with alternate colours. Neon purple seas, orange tree stumps and red clouds. She could never work fast enough. Everything at home was covered in paint... it still is." She missed the chaos, the rush, the smell of oil paint.

"We would love to see her work! Do you still have some?" Lou asked enthusiastically.

"I have her last collection, but it wasn't finished. The gallery still wanted it, but I couldn't break it up. It's still in her studio."

"It's hard to give up the things that made them who they were," Mrs Klaus agreed, and Lou took her hand. "I still lay out Henry's clothes every day – a habit I can't seem to break."

"And you don't have to," Lou said, comforting her mother.

Witnessing such an intimate moment of grief between them was an honour. Lyla's heart warmed, knowing they had each other, Kevin and Mason. She never wanted anyone to grieve alone as she had.

A knock on the door interrupted the moment, and Mrs Klaus straightened in her chair and wiped her eyes. "I'm not going to ruin my mascara," she said, forcing a smile.

"I'll see who it is," Lyla said.

"I'll help you get into your dress, Lou," Mrs Klaus said while Lyla put down the make-up brush to answer the door. Mason stood on the other side with a box in his hand, secured with a cream bow.

"I have something for you," he said, looking over her robe-covered body. "Are you wearing my robe?" He looked rather pleased about it.

"Yes – it's cosy," she reasoned. "Was there something else?" She stepped closer. "Or are you going to ask me what's underneath it?"

He raised his eyebrows and smirked. "For such a statement, I could keep you home tonight. We would have the whole house to ourselves."

Lyla shook her head, trying not to blush. "You could, but you can't. What do you need?"

"You can't go tonight without a dress."

"I'm going to borrow something of Sara's," she began, but Mason thrust the box towards her.

"And why would you have to wear hers when you have your own?" He smiled.

She held it in her arm and made to undo the bow.

"Wait – you can open it with the others. They should get a kick out of it."

"Please don't tell me it's the orange atrocity," she groaned, though she was still happy he had gone to the trouble of getting her something.

"You'll have to open it and see, but I think you'll be pleasantly surprised," he said, stepping towards her.

"I'm intrigued." She stilled as he gently kissed her cheek.

"I'll see you tonight," he said, and she smiled.

"Tonight then." He was already walking down the hall.

"Mason," she called, and he turned with a slight frown. "Thank you."

"You haven't seen it yet," he pointed out with a grin that made her stomach flip.

"Regardless, thank you."

Lyla closed the door and put the box on the bed as Mrs Klaus and Lou gathered around her.

"Mason bought you a dress?" Lou said, all astonishment.

Lyla shrugged. "He paid for something while we were in the dress shop, but I figured it was for his own suit, since we didn't take anything with us." She caught the glance Mrs Klaus gave her daughter.

"He's never been one for surprises – not good ones, anyway," Mrs Klaus said nervously.

"Pranks, on the other hand..." Lou said, and Lyla hesitated, suddenly worried something in the box was about to jump out at her. "I'm only teasing. Open it before I die of old age."

Lyla undid the bow and pushed it aside. Lifting the lid, she gasped when she saw the beautiful satin dress she had worn in the dress shop.

"It's beautiful," Mrs Klaus marvelled. "Who knew my son had such good taste."

"It's perfect," Lyla whispered as she removed the tissue and pulled it from the box. Perfect because it was no longer red, but a deep shade of green. *My favourite colour.*

"Strange he didn't pick something red – that's our family crest colour," Lou commented, but Lyla brushed a stray tear from beneath her glasses, trying to rid herself of the overwhelming emotions.

"Green is my favourite colour. It was red; he must have had it dyed." She couldn't believe he'd remembered such a small detail from her home.

"I don't think that's possible. I say he had it made," Mrs Klaus said.

"I thought *that* wasn't possible in such a short time."

"The dressmaker can be bribed easily with an extra helping of gold dust." Mrs Klaus winked.

"That's not against the law, is it? I don't want you to get in trouble," Lyla said, worried they would be putting themselves at risk.

"No – simply frowned upon. But there's nothing wrong with a bit of extra luck," Lou said, putting her at ease.

She held the dress against herself, the fabric silky against her fingertips. She didn't know how she was going to thank him, but she was sure she could think of something they would both enjoy.

CHAPTER TWENTY-ONE

Argyle, dressed in a three-piece suit, was waiting in the sleigh outside the house. The rest of the family had already gone ahead in another sleigh; Lyla had been delayed finishing off the details of Mrs Klaus's and Lou's make-up and hairstyles. After hours of small talk and a glass of champagne, she felt like she now had a mother and a sister, which both thrilled and terrified her.

Lyla caught sight of Mason out on the porch; he stared at her for a moment, his mouth agape.

"I'm almost ready," she called to him. He nodded, before returning his attention to Argyle. Lyla could just about hear their conversation as she put in her earring, looking in the mirror by the door.

"Any luck on the ring? I was hoping to return it to her tonight."

Lyla's guilt returned. She hadn't meant to lose it, but it was sweet he was trying to return it to her.

"I checked. Nothing was handed in to the jewellers, and those who cleaned up after the competition said they didn't see anything," Argyle said, deflated.

"Pity. I was so sure someone would have turned it in," Mason said, "but we tried."

"Since I couldn't help with the ring I thought a special drive would make up for it," Argyle said, and Lyla peered out to see the twinkling lights and tinsel decorating the sleigh.

"I noticed you've gone all out – I appreciate the effort. I want Lyla to have a good time. After what happened at the gingerbread competition, I think we owe her that," Mason told the old man, and Lyla turned back to the mirror before he noticed her watching. The kindness in his voice made her want to drag him inside and lock the door.

"Not every year we get a new Klaus. You and the missus have to arrive in style!" Argyle agreed.

She couldn't delay any longer; she removed her glasses. She'd have to settle for less than perfect sight tonight.

She stepped out and waited at the door. Mason was facing the sleigh, but Argyle cleared his throat and he glanced over his shoulder. Lyla pulled her dark curls to one side and laughed at his awed expression.

I can't wait for him to discover how little I'm wearing beneath it. She couldn't wear a bra, since the back was a series of tiny straps; luckily, she had more hips than bust.

"You're perfect. I didn't have your measurements, so I went off the size of the other dress," he said in a flurry. She didn't think she would ever get used to his compliments.

"I love it. I can't believe you had it done in green," she said, and his shoulders relaxed. Seeing him lose his composure was the best Christmas gift he could have given her.

"It's your favourite. I thought, since this isn't the Christmas you expected, I could give you something you'd love," he said, taking her hand and leading her towards the sleigh. She watched him, amazed at how open he was being. She knew in that moment that he had given her more than one thing to love.

"I don't think I've ever seen you smile in a suit. You should do it more often," she said, admiring the black suit he wore.

"I'll take note," he said, closing the gap between them. She noticed his gingerbread bowtie was slightly crooked.

"The bowtie is the perfect finish," she said, straightening it. She needed to do something so she wouldn't crumble under his uncompromising gaze.

"You both look wonderful. Now, we have a gala to get to," Argyle said, jumping into the driver's seat.

"Sorry – didn't mean to keep you waiting," Lyla said, flustered, and Argyle laughed.

"Or if you'd prefer, I can leave you both here?" he asked, and Mason scowled at him.

"We're going now," Mason assured him, and Lyla couldn't meet his eye.

He kissed her just enough to make her spend the rest of the evening wanting more, then offered her a hand, and she lifted her dress to step into the sleigh. Once the heavy blankets sheltered them from the falling snow, they set off along the lit paths. Lyla felt like she had officially slipped into a fairytale.

All the villagers turned to look at them as they entered the town hall, and Lyla couldn't help but feel overwhelmed. Thankfully music was already playing, with some people dancing down the middle of the room, so the attention on them was quickly diverted. She gazed at the chandelier, glistening with hanging glass snowflakes. With the white tablecloths, ice sculptures, and icy blue tapestries hanging from the windows, the theme was clearly a winter wonderland. *Mrs Klaus did a wonderful job arranging the room; it looks nothing like when Mason brought me here to see the council.* Then it had been dark and gloomy, but with the added chandeliers, everything glistened with warmth. She squeezed Mason's hand a little too tight and heard him chuckle. If she held his hand, she couldn't fidget.

"There's no need to be nervous. Everyone will love you," he said, but she doubted it.

She glanced about the room for the rest of the family, only for her eyes to settle on Natalie – who was wearing a red sequinned gown that moulded to her frame. *Wearing the Klaus colour is daring, but why am I not surprised?* She stood by an ice sculpture shaped like a Christmas tree with who Lyla guessed were her family. None of them looked pleased to see Lyla in attendance.

"You can't leave my side all night, or I'll kill you in your sleep," she warned Mason with a smile.

"I love your threats. Sadly, I must make a speech. Wait for me," he whispered, and just like that he was gone from her side, making his way through the dancing couples to the podium at the head of the room.

Feeling entirely out of place, and with no one to talk to, Lyla drifted through the crowd in hopes of running into a familiar face. Much to her relief, she spotted Mrs Klaus at a table not far from the podium and quickly made her way over.

She didn't have time to greet Mrs Klaus, because when she sat down a round of applause greeted Mason at the podium. Silence fell over the room.

Lyla noted the hope in the villagers' eyes as they looked up at him. Then again, their fate rested in his decision.

She was glad she hadn't eaten since lunch, or her stomach would have been twisted in knots. Even she didn't know what his decision would be. She couldn't help thinking about the email she'd sent Sam, and how foolish she had been, but there wasn't much time to fret as Mason began to address the room.

"Good evening, all – I promise I won't keep you long. This year we celebrate the season with heavy hearts, but despite our sorrow, my father – your friend – would have wanted us to celebrate, just as we have every year. On this night, he wouldn't want tears in his name. So I ask you to dance and sing in his honour, make this a Christmas he can watch over with a proud smile."

He cleared his throat, putting the paper in his hand in his pocket. "Many of you have questions about what this loss means for us. There must be a Klaus, and your next in line has been away for the last few years. This is a decision I don't make lightly, and this responsibility is my family's alone." A tense silence fell over the room, the crowd hanging on to his every word. "I'm happy to tell you all that I have decided to take my father's position as Klaus. I ask each of you for your help in making this transition. I have much to learn, but in returning," he caught Lyla's eye, "I have been reminded how important family is. How important Yule is to me, as it was to my father. Now, I ask you all if you'll accept me." There was a loud cheer and applause, which eventually settled down. "Then I ask you to raise your glass to my father, and to the seasons we will serve together."

Once the drinks were downed, Mason stepped down from the podium and was swallowed by the crowd, eager to shake his hand and hug him.

"Let the night begin," he called, and the orchestra started to play as he reached Lyla and his family.

Mrs Klaus was the first to embrace her son, tears in her eyes. "Thank you, son. He'd have been so very proud of you," she said, kissing his cheek.

"I'll do my best," he assured her, and Mrs Klaus cupped his face before wiping her tears away and giving him another squeeze.

"He's all yours now. I have some dancing to do!" she told Lyla, handing Mason over.

"You're full of surprises," Lyla said to him, reaching up on her tiptoes to kiss his cheek. "They're lucky to have you."

"I wouldn't have made the decision if it weren't for you. While you were getting ready, I read the last letter my father wanted to send. He knew his heart was going to give out; he was asking me to return. To make peace." He swallowed, and she rested a hand on his chest, trying to ease his sorrow. "If you'd let me burn them, I'd never have known how he felt," he admitted.

"Careful, my ego wouldn't survive saving Christmas," she teased, trying to hide her own happy tears.

Mason bent his head towards her. He was about to kiss her when someone cleared their throat at her back.

"May I have the next dance? It's about to begin," Natalie said brightly.

Lyla wished one of the icicles decorating the ceiling would fall and impale her. She smiled at the thought and released her partner to his ex. With the room watching the exchange, she couldn't say no. Even if the bitch *had* tried to poison her.

"If my fiancée doesn't mind," Mason teased. He squeezed her hand in warning, but the look he gave her told her he wanted an out.

"Who am I to separate old friends?" she said brightly, enjoying his discomfort.

Natalie winced, then smirked. "Ha – you're more generous than me. I wouldn't be able to take my hands off him if he were mine."

"Then it's a good thing he isn't," Lyla said with a false smile.

Mason took a drink from the table and downed it while Natalie's flurry of fake laughter surrounded them. "Shall we?" he asked. From the glance he gave Lyla, he didn't want to.

"I won't keep him long. The waiters have some hors d'oeuvres – be sure to stay away from the chocolate strawberries," Natalie warned with mock concern.

"You're too kind," Lyla forced herself to say, and left them as the music began.

Kevin came to walk with her to the buffet table. "She really is a nasty bit—"

"Don't!" Lyla cut him off, afraid of who might hear.

The food was enticing: mini iced cakes topped with gold; exquisitely laid out cheese and fruit platters; steaming meat or vegetable pies with flaky pastry, accompanied by baby potatoes, vegetables or salad. Though it all looked very tempting, Lyla was too distracted to eat.

"What? She is! She's been trying to get into this family since they were kids. Then our fathers arranged their marriage so Mason would have to stay," Kevin said, taking one of the chocolate-dipped strawberries she'd been warned about. "If it hadn't been for her meddling, Mason wouldn't have had such a massive fight with Dad."

Lyla could hear the anger in his words. She understood; he had lost his brother for years, and now his father.

"It's all in the past – and she lives here," she pointed out. "You can't hate her forever. If the marriage was arranged by their fathers, what was she to do?"

Kevin grinned. "Can't I? Wait! Mason hasn't told you

the whole story!" He shuffled in close so no one could overhear them gossip. "It was Natalie's idea. She insisted on the match – went to her father. She argued that since they were already a couple, they should be engaged. Mason tried to reason with her, but she pressed the issue with her parents. Our father agreed in order to keep Mason here, and her father wanted his daughter to be a Klaus."

Their conversation was interrupted by a few guests gossiping at the other end of the table. "How wonderful Mason and Natalie look together! It was such a pity their engagement ended." The other villagers nodded in agreement, watching the dancing couple in awe.

Lyla's skin itched as though she had eaten a strawberry, reminded of how she was an outsider.

Kevin, having heard the guests, offered her a mockingly deep bow and extended his hand. "May I have this dance, m'lady?"

Distracted by his grand display, Lyla curtseyed with a laugh, and took his hand. "It would be my honour."

"Don't worry about what they said. Some in the village have a hard time accepting the new and forgetting the past."

Appreciating his kind words, Lyla followed his lead to the dance floor.

"Careful of those hands, Kev," Mason warned with a wink as they passed. Kevin stuck his tongue out at his brother.

"What if they're right, though?" Lyla asked, watching Natalie pushing herself up against Mason. She wished the song would finally end – though Mason's strained expression was enough to make it worthwhile.

"You have nothing to worry about," Kevin said, glancing at the couple. "Mason hasn't taken his eyes off you the entire time."

"Regardless, I have you in my corner to save me," Lyla said, and Kevin beamed. Clearly, he liked the idea of being named her knight in shining armour.

"You're family now, and Klauses always protect each other," he said.

She smiled back at him, then looked around the room. She saw Lou and Sara together and Mrs Klaus talking with June, and for the first time since her mum had passed away, she felt like she was home.

The song ended. The orchestra was swapped out for a younger band, and the dancing became less formal. Unexpectedly, Mason twirled Lyla out of Kevin's arms and kissed her desperately. The sudden affection made her cheeks redden, and he looked rather pleased with himself.

"It seems the mulled wine has gone to your head – or is it me making you blush?" he teased, and she rolled her eyes, not caring where Natalie had gone.

"Glad to have you back."

"Happy to be back," he said, holding her close, though she could hear some sadness in the words.

"And you feel guilty about it," she suggested, knowing how hard it was to enjoy happy moments when you were grieving.

"Yes. But right now, all I want to do is dance with you," he said, dipping her so low that she clung to him, afraid he would drop her.

"Get a room," Kevin called from beside them, before heading off to join his friends.

"So that's who he likes," Lyla said, following his gaze to the guitarist in the band.

Mason smiled, watching his brother nervously pull at his neck. "Seems so."

They danced until her feet ached and the pins had fallen from her hair. The night came to an end with a raffle of gifts and baked goods, followed by a speech by Councilman Frederick. The room clapped once the speech was over.

Lyla turned to Mason, nodding towards the doors. The room grew stuffy, and she was in desperate need of air.

"Let's go outside," Mason whispered in her ear, and she followed his lead eagerly.

With their coats on, they stepped out of the noise and into the quiet, starry night. They walked through the quiet town, shrouded in fairy lights.

"Now that you've decided to take your father's seat, have you figured out what you want for the rest of your life?" Lyla asked, influenced heavily by the wine, holding onto his arm.

He stopped to look in a shop window, where a photo of his father was displayed to honour his memory. Lyla couldn't help but notice that the strength exuding from the picture was the same she felt when Mason entered a room. Add some grey to Mason's hair, and a short beard, and she could have been staring at a picture of him.

"Yes," he said, looking at her reflection in the window.

She didn't know what to say. *I have to go home, and he's taken his place amongst his family.* She tried to walk on, to silence her thoughts, but her heel caught on a cobblestone, twisting her ankle.

"Damn it," she cried out as the pain shot up her leg. Thankfully it dissipated quickly, but Mason scooped her up into his arms. Face to face, her arms around his neck, she couldn't help but wonder how she had never noticed how utterly exquisite he was. Dark eyes, a small scar on the bridge of his nose, full lips – *How could I have not seen you for months?* She inched closer to those lips, eager to taste them, when he cleared his throat. *Does he not want to kiss me? Was last night a mistake?*

Before she could send herself further into a spiral, she realised a family was passing them.

"Merry Christmas, Mr Klaus," the family chorused, and Lyla wanted to bury herself in his jacket.

"Have a good evening," Mason called after them, before whispering into her ear, "I didn't realise you were so desperate to kiss me that you would do it in front of children."

She slapped his chest, almost knocking herself from his arms, and then suddenly felt like they had come full circle. *This is how we arrived in the village – and now we're so close to leaving.*

Leaving... She stared up at him as he pulled her closer. *Will I be leaving alone?*

Mason's kiss made her wish she never had to.

CHAPTER TWENTY-TWO

"Let's get these off you before you break your neck," Mason said with a devilish smile and the door to the spare room locked.

Lyla sat on the bed, watching him undo the clasps on her heels. One of his hands took off a shoe while the other travelled higher up her leg, pushing up her dress to expose her legs.

"I need a better view to see what I'm doing," he said seriously, stopping to kiss a freckle on her knee.

"I think you know exactly what you're doing," she said, looking down at him as he kissed the other knee, then went to work on the other heel, removing it with ease. She tried to focus on the flames dancing in the fireplace – on anything but the sensation of his hands on her bare skin, so good she was sure it would overwhelm her. "And you never need to stop," she added, leaning forward, revealing her cleavage.

His head snapped up from the shoe. Lyla was very aware that he could see her nipples through the thin satin material.

"You might regret saying that." Mason pushed her legs apart so that he could kneel between them.

"Why?" she asked.

His hands slid higher up her thighs until he gripped her underwear, and her breath grew tight as he stopped there, twisting the lace tight in his fists. She gripped the back of his neck and brought his lips to hers. A crushing kiss that threatened to bruise her, but she loved every second. She gasped and shuddered when his hand brushed over her satin-covered breast.

"Because I won't ever tire of your body, and I'm afraid we might die in this bed with your legs wrapped around me," he told her.

He pulled her hips sharply against his, and she could feel how much he wanted her. Her desire flared, threatening to burn her alive. She had no awareness of anything except his lips on hers, his hands beneath her dress, gripping her hips almost painfully.

"With my name on your lips," he added in her ear, and her core clenched.

"Then I'll die satisfied," she replied, moving her hips against his, and a groan escaped him.

His lips hungrily devouring hers, he teasingly undid the thin straps on the back of her dress. "I only bought you this dress so I could take it off."

Her nipples hardened as he caressed one breast and then the other, pinching and pulling until she bit his lip in protest. He hissed and pulled back, licking the blood on his lip, though the desire only burned hotter in his eyes.

"Sorry," she sighed, only to realise she was mostly exposed while he was still fully dressed. She undid the buttons on his shirt, exposing his strong chest and broad shoulders she couldn't wait to sink her teeth into. He laughed at her searching eyes.

"Something you're looking for?" he asked, as breathless as she was.

"You're still wearing far too many clothes."

His lips found her neck while his hand slipped between her legs, his thumb grazing her underwear, and she gasped as he ever so gently teased her. Pride darkened his eyes as he realised how wet she was.

"You're making it very hard to concentrate," she said, working on his belt but finding she had little control of her hands, or her body.

"Let me make it easier for you then." He stripped off his trousers and boxers. It turned her on watching his expression as he exposed all of himself for her pleasure. She felt less self-conscious once he stood as vulnerable as she was.

"You've made me hard from the moment you stepped into my office. In your oh-so-tight skirts and heels," he admitted.

"I thought you hated me," she gasped as her lace underwear was discarded.

"Hating you only made me want to fuck you all the more." He pulled her to her feet, and she stepped out of the dress. She tried to catch her breath from the rush of pleasure as his fingers slipped between her legs, and she bit her lip to silence a moan.

"Is that all you want to do? Fuck me?" she asked playfully. He kissed her neck, her breasts, her stomach, easing her onto the bed.

He pinned her arms above her head. She couldn't move, couldn't avoid his dark eyes.

"No." The words caught in his throat. "I want to make you mine."

"You have me," she promised, and he released her hands, which she wrapped around his neck as he lavished her with kisses.

She needed him – more of him than she thought he could give. Every impulse in her wanted to move, to feel the friction of her body against his, but he waited until she was writhing beneath him as his fingers explored and teased the part of her that wanted him so desperately.

She clawed at his skin. "Please," she begged. He groaned as she moved her hips against his until he gave in and buried himself inside her.

"Don't move," he pleaded. She tried to control herself, but the sensation of his body against hers made her lose control. She arched her back as he pushed deeper.

"Again," she pleaded, and he obeyed. She shivered beneath him, and she knew she wouldn't last long after being teased for so long. She grabbed his hips and urged him to keep moving.

"Don't stop," she panted, and he didn't. Not until they both shattered in each other's arms.

Lyla woke to find Mason's side of the bed empty and the fire out.

She pulled on his shirt from the night before tiptoeing down the hallway. The light at the end of the corridor and slightly open office door told her he might be inside. She peered inside cautiously in case she was disturbing Mrs Klaus, but found herself staring at Mason's shirtless back as he stood in front of the fireplace.

She sneaked in behind him and wrapped her arms around his waist. He went rigid as she kissed his back.

"You're going to freeze like this," she said, holding him tightly, but he said nothing. When he didn't return the embrace, she released him. "Are you alright? Come back to bed." She moved to stand beside him, and only then noticed the papers in his hand. *Transfer of shares,* read the first line.

Her heart threatened to stop.

"You not only used me, but you risked revealing an ancient secret over a damn *contract*?" Mason snapped, throwing the papers onto the floor.

"Wh-why were you reading my email?" she stammered, her hands clasped in front of her to stop herself from reaching for him.

"Reading your email? You mean Sam's email? You mean the email where you planned to take the company for yourself? I came in to get the letters my father left me – I wanted to read them with you, to *share* them with you. I saw the laptop was on, and I thought it was something to do with the company." His stark expression frightened her.

"I thought I deleted it! I won't talk to you when you're this angry," she declared, but he blocked her path.

"Deleted it? That's all you care about – hiding your trail? Well, it's a good thing he sent another. When you didn't reply, he thought you hadn't received it."

Lyla cursed herself for her stupidity. *Why didn't I tell Sam that I'd changed my mind?*

"I was going to divide the company equally! How foolish of me to think we could be equal partners, when you've been scheming this whole time, using the death of my father against me." He was holding his hand over his heart as if to protect it from her.

"When you brought me here, I thought you would stay – that you might not return. You would have to leave the company in order to stay. I was never going to show you these!"

"And when did you decide this? When did you have this epiphany of your feelings for me? Was it before or after you decided to blackmail me out of the company?" he hissed, backing her up against the desk. She knew he would have seen the time stamp on the email.

"Yesterday morning. I deleted it before the Gala. I decided while we were in the cabin, when you saved me from the wolves, that I couldn't go through with it. I was wrong about you. Please don't make more of this than it is!"

The hurt in his eyes was enough to shatter her.

"You were wrong about me, but I was right about you. Entitled, selfish, out for no one but herself," he snapped.

She felt like she had been punched. "The company was mine before you came."

"And I was SAVING it for you!" he shouted, and she lost control of her temper.

"Saving it? There's barely anything left of how I remember it! Just because you turned your back on your legacy doesn't mean you get to take mine."

She regretted the words as soon as they left her mouth, even if there was some truth to them. He stared at her in silence as the weight of all that had gone unsaid between them came crashing down.

There was a knock on the door. Lyla wiped the tears from her eyes and turned her back to the door, not wanting whoever entered to see she was upset.

"Are you both okay?" Mrs Klaus said, looking like she was still half-asleep.

"We were..." Lyla started.

"Her cat got into some papers. We were cleaning up," Mason said to his mother, without so much as a glance towards Lyla.

"Alright… no need to get so upset over a cat. We can tidy up in the morning," Mrs Klaus said uncertainly, looking down at the scattered paper on the floor. Lyla was sure it hadn't escaped her notice that Jones wasn't in the office.

Mrs Klaus left them, and Lyla tried to gather her thoughts, tried to think of what to say to make him understand.

"You need to leave," was all he said once the door closed.

"We can talk about this; I know you don't want to end this. Please hear me out – you can't put this space between us. Not when we've come so far," she pleaded, taking his hand.

Mason only shook her off. "You did this to us. You."

His icy glare was enough to make her flee to her room before either of them said something that couldn't be forgiven. He was angry, grieving, and she had betrayed his trust. That was something he didn't give freely, and now she had shown him exactly what the cost was.

Curling up on her bed, Jones snuggled into her, Lyla waited for Mason to come, waited for the twist of the handle, hoping they could come back from this. But the hours ticked by and the door, remained stubbornly closed.

CHAPTER TWENTY-THREE

Lyla left the house at first light; she couldn't stand to be there a moment longer. The thought of having to suffer through breakfast with Mason was unbearable.

She found herself sitting in the Peppermint & Pumpkin Coffee Shop, trying to think of what to do. The strong smell of coffee and peppermint was an assault to the senses, but she was won over by the giant mugs in the shape of pumpkins, and the assortment of cakes in the glass case at the counter.

"Lyla! How good of you to come and see us," someone said from behind the counter. It took Lyla a moment to register that the older woman in a pumpkin-covered apron was June.

"I thought I would pop in for some breakfast," she explained, wishing she had gone to a coffee shop where no one knew her.

"Mason isn't with you?" June asked, looking toward the door.

"He had to get to the workshop," Lyla lied. June seemed to suspect nothing.

"There are some books on the shelves that might interest you, if you need some company," she offered, but Lyla didn't think she could focus on anything, let alone words on a page. She ordered herself a coffee. Since she was going to be here a while, she asked for some breakfast too, needing all the strength she could get for the day ahead.

It was busier than she had expected at such an early hour. Many of the patrons looked a little worse for wear after last night's festivities.

I could leave and forget everything that happened, she thought, but the words caused something inside her to twist so badly that she lost her breath. *Or I could talk to him and convince him to forgive me. He can't forget what's happened between us so quickly. His heart isn't that cold.*

Mason had told her that he had come here every day for lunch when he was working in the workshop as a teenager, so she waited. It was far too early, but she didn't want to linger at the house, and she couldn't sleep anymore. Every time the bell rang, her head snapped up, hoping it was him coming through the door. But after multiple coffees, and slices of cake, there was still no sign of him. She considered going to the workshop, but she didn't want to interrupt him or distract him while he was working. *Why did I have to go so far?* She thought of the email she had sent Sam, talking of a new CEO, calling him the Grinch. She cursed herself, taking a sip of her steaming peppermint latte.

"One decaf toffee nut cappuccino, please!" a familiar voice ordered at the counter, and Lyla looked up to see Lou looking at the cakes.

Lyla tensed, wondering if her brother had told Lou what had happened. She was tucked away in the corner of the cafe, so she figured she might not be spotted.

"Coming right up. I'll have it brought to you," June said, looking towards Lyla, and she knew her retreat was exposed.

Lou was coming towards her. *Has he told her what I did?* She glanced at the other patrons, not looking forward to being scolded in public – especially not in a place where everyone looked after each other. Her misdeed would certainly mark her for life. *Not that I'll be in Yule much longer.*

"I see you have the power to anger my brother even more than I do. He's been at the workshop since before dawn. I think we'll have enough Dust for the next two Christmases," Lou said, pulling up her chair beside Lyla. She was relieved for the honest conversation opener; she didn't think she could handle chitchat.

"We tend to bring out the worst in each other," she admitted, because it was true.

Lou eyed the black forest gateau in front of Lyla. "Are you going to eat that? They were sold out at the counter. With this hangover, I'm dying for a slice."

Lyla shook her head. She didn't even have the energy to think about her own hangover. *I deserve to suffer.*

"Go ahead. This would be my third slice anyway," she admitted, forcing herself to smile as she pushed the plate over to Lou.

"So you're the cake thief. How long have you been here?" Lou asked, digging in. Their conversation was interrupted by June bringing over Lou's order.

"Glad you finally arrived. She's been waiting for hours," June said, reprimanding Lou as she placed the coffee on the table.

"Have you really been here for hours?" Lou raised an eyebrow when June had left.

"Long enough to consume about three coffees – two decaf, I'm not insane – breakfast, and two slices of cake," she tallied.

"Impressive. Sounds like you're hiding?" Lou said, taking a sip of her coffee. The sweet smell made Lyla wish for another cup, but she didn't think her nervous system would thank her.

"More like waiting. Mason said he comes here for lunch," she admitted, hoping he would come through the door when the bell chimed. Then again, she didn't really fancy his sister being there for everything they had to say to each other.

"Are you going to tell me what happened? You've seen me half-naked, so we're practically sisters," Lou joked.

The memory of helping her get dressed for the gala and the thought of losing her friendship only made Lyla sadder.

"I... did something unforgivable. I tried to take it back. I never even did it, but I thought about it. Mason found out. It's a mess." She gripped her hair by the roots in frustration.

"How cryptic. But since you've been stuck here for the last ten days, how bad could it have been?" Lou asked, eager for more information.

Lyla couldn't bring herself to tell her more. Lou gave her a penetrating look.

"So, it was bad." She put down the fork, giving Lyla her full attention. "Are you going to talk to him? When you do see him?"

"I think I'm the last person he wants to talk to. Coming back was hard enough for him. When I agreed to come, I thought I was making it easier for him. Instead, I made it so much worse," she said, thinking she should have closed the door on him the day after the fire.

"It was hard for him? He didn't seem that bothered."

"Like you wouldn't believe. When he got your letter, he got exceptionally drunk and I had to bring him home – without any shoes, I might add. Before then we barely spoke to each other except to yell..." Lyla froze, realising she had revealed their secret. She sat in silence, waiting for Lou to speak.

Lou squeezed her hand, a silent way of saying it was okay, and Lyla let out a grateful breath.

"Don't worry. I knew the first time we had breakfast together that you weren't a couple. Though I thought there was serious potential when he went after you and brought you to the cabin."

"Sorry if we've upset you, or your family, by lying. I should never have come. I should never have let him talk me into it. Things were hostile but functioning before, and now I just don't know..."

"Are you serious? You made a miserable Christmas so much better. Distraction is the kindest thing you could have done for my brother – for Mum. She's been so busy thinking about you two, she's had a much-needed break from her grief. I worry about what will happen when the season ends, which is why I was hoping Mason would stay."

"I don't know what he'll do now. He said he would stay last night, I hope what happened between us won't change his mind. He seems so much happier here than he did back in the city."

"His happiness has more to do with who he's with than where he is. Of that, I can assure you..." Lou hesitated, taking another sip of coffee. "But, as the eldest in the family, I do have to ask. If you could stay here, would you? Being with a Klaus is a lifetime commitment. You even being here is breaking our laws. I didn't say anything because I saw how close you were getting. He even brought you before everyone in the council, and to the gala. For an outsider, you must realise how important that is to us. If you could patch things up, could you see yourself staying here? Becoming one of us?"

Lyla could see the stress in Lou's eyes and the worry their situation had caused her, which only furthered her guilt, because she didn't know how to answer her.

"I don't know," she admitted.

Lou looked disappointed, clicking her fingernail against the edge of her coffee cup.

"It's not because I don't love it here. This place is like a dream come true – except for the wolves that tried to eat me."

Lou chuckled at that, and the tension between them dissolved.

"Back home, there's never been much for me except for the legacy of the family company. I was so focused on carrying on that legacy, making my own name in it, that I put it before everything else. To leave it behind, leave my friends, and have to lie to them... Giving up the home my mum raised me in..."

Lyla realised how much of what she was saying sounded like a no. Yet, despite it all, she would do any of those things if Mason forgave her.

Chapter Twenty-Four

The conversation with Lou turned to less fraught topics, such as how she'd met Sara, but she soon had to head back to work. Lyla asked whether she could join her in the workshop in the hope of seeing Mason, only to discover that the mechanics worked on the sleighs in another part of Yule.

She decided to wander around the village for a while, if only to prevent herself from eating more cake. Eventually she stopped by the workshop, determined to face her problems. Inside, she searched for any familiar face amongst the bustle, and found Ian fixing a tap on the hourglass.

"Ian, sorry to disturb you," she said, tapping his shoulder. He jumped and she apologised.

"Lost in my own world," he said, putting down his wrench. "What can I do for you?"

"I was looking for Mason," she began, glancing around the busy workshop. Everyone was too busy preparing for the last dash of the season to even notice she had come in. "I didn't mean to interrupt you..."

"Not at all – I've been working on this tap for a bloody hour. It won't budge, and I could do with a break." He scratched the back of his head and looked up at the office. "But it's not me you want to see. Sorry to say, but Mason already left for the day. Said something about checking the sleighs."

"Oh. I must have passed him," Lyla said, trying not to sound too disappointed.

"Is everything all right? I can tell him you were here when he returns," he offered.

"Fine, nothing to worry about. Just wanted to see him. There's no need to mention." She turned to leave, but she had to ask. "Do you know where he might be?"

Ian picked up his wrench. "I can't say I do." He gave her a sympathetic look before going back to the tap.

"Thank you. I won't keep you any longer," she said, leaving him to his work. The last thing she wanted was for Mason to think she was involving others in their drama.

By the time she reached the house, she was frozen through and desperate for a seat by the fire and a cup of tea. The rest of the family were out, and there was still no sign of Mason having been in the office or the spare room.

When she reached their bedroom, the room had been cleaned and her suitcase sat on the bed.

Lyla wrapped her arms around herself, as though trying to protect herself from what the gesture meant. *He wants me gone.* She suppressed the urge to cry, afraid that if she let the tears fall, they would never stop. Picking up a pillow, she hugged it to her chest. Last night they'd shared a bed, and today he was telling her to leave.

She lifted the lid of the case to find the dress she had worn last night, and a sheaf of papers on top. She picked them up, confused, and realised it was a new contract. *He must have drawn it up and left it here while I was out.* She picked up the pages and brought them towards the fire, ready to destroy them, then caught sight of Mason's signature. Flicking through the pages, she realised that the company shares were hers – but this wasn't how she wanted to earn her legacy. She wanted to save the company, and she needed his help, needed him. She couldn't do everything herself, nor did she want to anymore. She threw the contract into the fire and picked up the suitcase, ready to put it under her bed. To hide it, before anyone else saw.

He thinks I'm that easy to get rid of? I'm not leaving. He'll talk to me whether he wants to or not. Lyla heard the door open behind her, and hope swelled in her chest.

"Mason?" she asked, but something hard struck the side of her head, and the room went dark.

Lyla woke on a wooden floor with a blinding headache. Instantly, she checked her head for bleeding, but there was only a bump. She picked up her glasses, which were lying beside her, before looking up to find she was sitting in the town hall. Gone was any trace of the gala. The council sat before her, all looking either murderous or sympathetic.

"The accused was packing a suitcase. She was going to flee, and who knows what she would have said if I had let her leave! I did what I had to in order to bring her here." Standing next to her, Natalie addressed the council.

Now it was Lyla's turn to look murderous. *The bitch knocked me out? What type of person bashes someone over the head? She could have asked to talk, like a sane person.* Lyla struggled to her feet, a little dizzier than she'd expected to be.

"Was such force necessary?" a familiar voice asked, and Lyla searched the council to find Mrs Klaus sitting amongst them. To Lyla's relief, she looked more sympathetic than the rest. In fact, when Mrs Klaus's gaze flicked to Natalie, she looked horrified.

"You couldn't kill me with the strawberries, so you want to force the council to wipe my memory? Because if I forget about what happened here, I'll forget my feelings for Mason. Is a guy really worth it?" Lyla demanded.

"This has nothing to do with Mason," Natalie declared, stamping her foot on the hardwood floor like a petulant child.

"Killing you with strawberries? Attempting to force the council's hand? Those are some strong accusations," Frederick said, and Lyla felt utterly doomed. Now that Mason was going to take his father's seat, it meant Frederick wouldn't be the next Klaus. He didn't look pleased about it.

"I don't accuse Natalie of anything that isn't true. However, I don't hold it against her. I just want to leave Yule with my memories," she said to the council.

"Then what do you suggest we do? Natalie claims you have entered Yule under false pretences – that you are in fact not engaged to Mason Klaus. Such deception warrants action," Una said, and dread spread through Lyla's veins like lava.

"You can't truly mean to wipe my memory? I'd never tell anyone about this place. You've all been so kind to me – except for knocking me unconscious and dragging me here against my will." That addition earned her no favours; the council shook their heads. She didn't want to deny the claims outright, but nor did she want to admit to them, for Mason's sake.

"If you have nothing to hide, then why the facade? Why did you come here if it was all a lie?" Frederick asked.

Lyla looked at Natalie. "How did you find out?"

"I was bringing some breakfast to the workshop, and I overheard Mason and Mrs Klaus talking. Mason admitted they aren't engaged, and she won't be coming back to Yule once this season ends. As much as it pains me to hurt the Klaus family, I had to bring it to the attention of the council," Natalie said with feigned sorrow.

"Yes, I can see how much it pains you," Lyla muttered under her breath.

Natalie opened her mouth to answer, but Mrs Klaus held up her hand, silencing her.

"Yes. I did talk to my son, and yes, they are not engaged. However, harming Lyla is deplorable. If you had an issue, you should have come to me or Mason, and we could have discussed this privately."

"Would you prefer your son's deception of this council remain hidden?" Frederick asked in horror.

"Klauses don't hide from anything. My son had his reasons, and Lyla has done nothing to warrant harm. I believe her to be a trustworthy person, regardless of how she came to be here," Mrs Klaus said. Lyla wanted to thank her, but now was not the time. "I'm surprised at you, Natalie; I didn't think you would eavesdrop on a private conversation."

"Regardless of how Natalie found out, and your trust in the woman who has been living under your roof, how can we, Yule, trust a single word Lyla says? I say we vote. This isn't about one lie, but about the safety of our people," Frederick said, and there was a murmur of agreement.

Mrs Klaus rose from the table. "We are not going to do anything except let this woman return home!"

Frederick banged on the gavel. "You can't make decisions for the council. It was your son who betrayed our trust after all!"

Mrs Klaus's face fell in shame, and Lyla's heart ached for the woman, who had already lost so much.

Silence fell over the room as Mason walked through the doors, his expression fixed and cold. *This is the Mason I knew in the real world. Why doesn't he let the council deal with me?*

"Lyla had no intention of lying to the council," he announced. "This farce was my idea. Selfishly, I wanted a friend to accompany me home. Given our laws, there was only one way to bring her here. I convinced her to lie. She knew nothing of where I was bringing her, or what she was getting herself into."

Lyla watched as Natalie shrank under his imposing gaze. *She wasn't expecting Mason to defend me. How much did she hear of what happened?*

"If you want me to uphold my decision, to stay in the village and inherit my father's place, then Lyla must be allowed to leave," Mason concluded.

The council appeared much more concerned with the prospect of him leaving than with her exposing their secret.

"You can't hold this council hostage – this is not how it works," Frederick protested, puffing out his chest.

"This council wanted my return and the line of Klauses to continue. Here I am. But if you hold her, or sentence her, the line will end with me. My family will never serve those who take an innocent woman's memories, especially one I tricked into coming here." Mason continued, his voice inflexible, and the council listened.

If Lyla hadn't known better, she'd have thought they were back home in the boardroom, arguing about mandates and cutbacks. However, there was one major difference: this time he was fighting for her, not against her.

"Yes, he tricked me into coming here, but I could have left. The truth is, once I met his family, I didn't want to." She looked to Mason and swallowed the knot in her throat, surprised when he let her continue. "I haven't had a proper family in a long time. I forgot what it was like to sit around a table for a meal or argue about bowties and cooking. You have such a community here; you all look after each other and care for one another. You've won me over with peppermint lattes and magic. I'd never betray Yule's secret. Please let me keep my memories, because I'll cherish them forever," she said, trying not to let her emotions spill over.

Mason gave her a reassuring look, before redirecting an icy glare towards Natalie and the council.

An uncomfortable moment passed as the council digested her words. Lyla studied their expressions; some seemed to have softened towards her.

"Since you have Mrs Klaus's understanding, then we will trust her judgement. I only hope you are telling the truth and that you will value all that we have shared with you," Frederick said reluctantly. Lyla suspected he was trying to appease everyone.

The council around him muttered their agreement, and Lyla felt like a weight had been lifted from her shoulders. Mrs Klaus winked at her. Lyla stifled a tearful smile, knowing she had her support.

"Fine. She is of no consequence to us—" Frederick began.

Natalie tried to interrupt, her words a high-pitched plea, but a raised hand silenced her. She turned on Lyla, leaning over her.

"Keep your memories. I hope they haunt you," she snarled.

Lyla noticed that a thin gold chain had slipped from inside her blouse. At the end of the chain was her ring. The ring Mason had given her – the one she had lost. No, she hadn't lost it; Natalie had stolen it.

"They will, but what will comfort me is knowing that Mason will never love you," she said, snatching the ring. The chain snapped, and Natalie reared back. "I believe this belongs to *me.*"

Natalie gaped. She looked to the council, clearly hoping for them to intervene, but they did nothing. She stormed out of the hall in a huff. Lyla had never been so happy to see someone leave. She dropped the chain and clutched the ring in her palm, the relief of getting it back almost overshadowing what Frederick was saying.

"As I was saying, Lyla may leave – but you must never speak a word of this place, and you can never return."

Never return? Her stomach dropped. She wouldn't just be leaving Mason behind, but his family and the acquaintances she'd made. Since she'd arrived, she'd worried about hurting others, but she had never considered how much it would hurt *her* to leave them behind.

The gavel dropped, and the council was dismissed. Lyla watched Mrs Klaus leave. She wanted to go to her, to apologise and tell her how much she would miss her. To thank her for defending her and making her feel at home. She took a step forward, but Mason placed a hand on her shoulder, holding her in place.

"Follow me," Mason said. She thought his tone was less chilling than before. It gave her hope, so she did, out of the chamber and out into the heavily falling snow. She nearly knocked into him when he spun on his heels to face her. "I didn't mean for Nat to overhear my conversation; I was talking to Mum in private. She asked if we were together, and I said no. Figured there was no point in lying any longer."

Her heart ached.

"If I hadn't betrayed your trust then we wouldn't have got here," she said, desperately wanting to reach out for him. But Mason looked like he couldn't care less about her excuses. They might as well be back in the office, animosity lingering between them. She waited for him to speak, to say something.

"I never should have brought you here. It was a mistake." His words caused pain in places she didn't know existed.

"Can I say goodbye to your mum, to Lou and Kevin? I don't want them to think I left without any thought for them," she asked, though it came out as more of a plea. She also had to get Jones – she certainly wasn't going to leave him behind.

"You should leave, before they change their mind," was all he said.

A shred of hope stirred in her as he took her hand; then she felt the chill of metal and saw the gold bell he'd placed on her palm.

Before she could say anything, even if only to thank him for saving her life, Yule melted away around her. Before long, she was standing in her kitchen with Jones perched on the counter.

"How did you get here?" she gasped, when she noticed the small bell attached to his collar. *Mason really thought of everything*. Her chest tightened, as did her grip on the bell in her hand, and all she could do was cry.

CHAPTER TWENTY-FIVE

Lyla shook the bell in her hand, willing herself to return, but the bell didn't ring; it merely disintegrated in her hand. As though her time in the village, her time with Mason, had never happened. Her plugged in phone rang on the counter, distracting her from her tears.

12 missed calls? Some were from Sam, but most were from her father. *Maybe this marriage will end before the honeymoon,* she thought, sniffling – she didn't know if it was from the tears or how cold the house was. Once the boiler was lit, she dialled her dad's number, the international ring beeping. *So he is still on his honeymoon...* She silently prayed he wouldn't answer. All she wanted to do was crawl into bed and forget.

"Ly? Hello? I couldn't get you earlier. I think the signal here was stopping me from getting through," her dad said frantically. The line wasn't great, but she could make him out clearly enough.

"Sorry, I've been... busy the last few days. I kept meaning to get back to you, but I didn't want to interrupt your honeymoon. How's it going?" she asked as she boiled the kettle, desperate to warm herself.

"Bliss. The perfect way to spend the winter is in the sun and sand, but I didn't call to talk about the weather!"

She couldn't remember the last time she had heard him so happy. She was glad for him, although slightly jealous. "I gathered."

"Cut the attitude – you aren't too old for a scolding," he said, a smile in his voice, but she wasn't in the mood for humour.

The kettle whistled, and she put the phone on speaker so she could hold the mug of tea in her hands.

"Whatever it is, can it wait until tomorrow? I'm tired. It's the middle of the night here, and if it's nothing pressing..."

"No, wait. There's something urgent regarding the company. Mr Klaus sent me an email yesterday granting you his shares and giving his notice. Did you know about this? I would have appreciated a heads up. He won't be returning to the company in the new year. I didn't expect him to sort the finances so quickly! Then again, he came highly recommended."

She couldn't tell him *she* was the reason Mason was leaving, and she didn't want to either.

"I didn't know he was going to contact you, but I told you we weren't in so much trouble," she said, trying to keep her voice level.

He sighed, and she knew where the conversation was going.

"When I signed the papers granting him the majority, I did it to protect you. After our initial meeting, I knew the company couldn't continue as it was. I wanted you to take my place, but not my problems. Mr Klaus informed me our finances weren't secure; you could have ended up in a terrible position. He was willing to reinvest in the company – he even paid those who were laid off double their severance. When the factory closed, he made sure the workers were taken on by different factories. It took money to do that. Money which you could have only come up with by selling your mother's house, and she never would have wanted you to do that. Once the business was stable, it was written into his contract that he would leave."

She had known the company's situation, but she hadn't wanted to admit it – to admit how much she had needed Mason's help. But she hadn't known that he had personally invested in the company. She wished she had.

I did it to protect you. Mason's words cut through her as she realised he had done more for her than she knew. Collecting herself, she picked up her phone as her dad called her name.

"Sorry. I'm here. You should have told me before! Given me some say, some understanding. I wouldn't have seen him as an..."

"Enemy? Not for a minute. He was our miracle!" Lyla's dad laughed without a care in the world. "We'll talk again soon. I'm late for a date."

"Careful, Dad. Don't want to hear of wife number five before I've met number four."

"You wound me; you'd be lucky to have one husband. Being alone in that house isn't good for you."

She certainly didn't want to have *this* conversation. "It's not my fault you left once Mum was gone." She tried to make light of it, putting her empty mug in the copper sink.

"Honey, I didn't leave you. I moved on. Life is for the living, and I wish you would do the same—"

The phone cut off as they lost signal, and Lyla didn't have the energy to ring him back.

"What have I done?" she groaned, stroking Jones's ears as he purred into her chest. There was nothing she could do to change the past. Instead, she scooped the cat into her arms and went to bed, hoping everything would look brighter in the morning.

CHRISTMAS EVE

Lyla walked back through the city streets after escaping the buzz and merriment of Sam's annual Christmas Eve party. The only promising part of the night was discovering that the watermelon turkey wasn't being served. Sam had convinced her to go by saying that getting out of the house would make her feel less alone, but as she'd watched everyone celebrating the season, all she could think about was Yule and the kind people she had got to know. How she wouldn't see Lou again, or receive another hug from Mrs Klaus. She hadn't even had a chance to say goodbye to Kevin. She hadn't just lost Mason – she felt like she'd lost a family.

Despite the rain, she didn't hail a taxi; she needed the walk to clear her head.

Reaching the steps to her door, she searched in her tiny purse for her keys. Her fingers were so numb from the cold that she dropped them.

"Damn it," she groaned, reaching into the puddle and pulling them out.

"I thought you wouldn't be home," Mason said.

She jumped and turned. He was standing at the top of the steps.

"Jesus, you scared me to death. Don't sneak up on a girl at midnight!"

Then she realised who she was scolding, and was too surprised to speak again. She made her way slowly up the steps, afraid that if she spoke, if she moved too quickly, he would disappear.

"I think it's warranted, considering you tore my heart out," he said, though there was no malice in his voice.

"I'm sorry, but can we stand inside? I'm so cold," she begged, silently pleading for him not to leave. Once the door was open, she had to put Jones in the other room to stop him escaping. When she looked back, Mason was still standing in the entryway.

"Aren't you going to come in?" she asked, trying not to hope.

Mason shook his head. "No, I can't tonight. I don't have long."

She had to tell him how she was feeling. It was now or never.

"The last thing I wanted to do was hurt you. When I wrote that email to Sam, we weren't even friends. There was nothing between us. Or, at least, I *thought* there was nothing between us. I was so focused on having something of my own that I never considered sharing it with someone I love."

"Someone you love?" he asked, his eyes searching hers.

"I hate it when you're cold and distant, but yes, I love you! Before I only saw one side of you, but I didn't know everything you did for the company, the workers – for me.

I didn't know your heart before, and I'm sorry I never gave you a chance." Her words were so frantic she hardly knew what she was saying. All she knew was that she had to say it.

Mason left the entryway, disappearing out the door without a word, and she thought the floor would open beneath her feet. She forced herself to swallow the tears, but then heard footsteps again. Mason stood before her in the hall, a small red box in his hand tied with a bow.

"Don't worry, I'm not going to propose. I had to dry my feet on the mat," he explained. She stared at the box, furious at him for worrying about her flooring at a time like this.

"That was the last thing on my mind," she snapped. "I was thinking you were about to give me coal."

He smirked. "I wouldn't give you coal, though you're definitely on the naughty list. Open it?"

Lyla hesitated, unsure of whether it would be a gift or a curse. He still hadn't said anything in response to her admission, and it was killing her.

Mason rolled his eyes and undid the red ribbon. She followed his lead and opened the lid to find a silver bell inside.

"A bell?" she asked, picking it up and realising her initials were carved into the side: *LS*.

"I want you to come back with me. I spoke with the council and told them everything. Not about the contract, but about how much I need you. They agreed to your return. You had more than a few of the townspeople speak up for you," he told her.

"You forgive me?" she said, her words catching in her throat.

"You can thank my family for forcing me to see sense – but even without them fighting your corner... As soon as you were gone, it wasn't the same. You made a mistake, but

I made a worse one letting you go." He kissed her forehead, and she never wanted him to leave again.

But... leaving here? How can I?

"I... want to, more than anything, but I can't leave the company. There's no one else to run it," she whispered. "I can't disappear and put hundreds of people out of work."

"There's no need to worry about the company. I meant for you to come to Yule for New Year's. We'll be back in the office by the time everyone returns," he promised, reaching for her.

She stepped back, remembering her conversation with Lou in the coffee shop. As much as she wanted his forgiveness, his love, she didn't know if she could accept it.

"Staying in Yule is right for you, and as much as I'd love it, I don't know if it's right for me. I can't be a Mrs Klaus. I want to be yours, but the role your mother plays... I don't want to be a spare part – no disrespect to what your mother does," she said, not wanting to insult the family who had clearly defended her.

"I'm sure she'd wash your mouth out with peppermint. Yule, and my father, wouldn't have been able to function without her. But this is not about my parents' relationship – this is about us!"

"How can there be an us when you're Santa Claus?" Lyla didn't want to argue, but she had to ask the hard questions.

"Because you're going to run the company here, and I can come and go. My role is more figurative; I make sure everything in Yule is running smoothly. I'll make it work – delegate. Frederick was more than happy to keep things running this evening so that I could be here. Though he isn't all too pleased with my choice of Mrs Klaus, he was overjoyed at having my position for the night. Lou is going to continue running the workshops; she does it more efficiently than I do anyway. Kevin will start working with the reindeer next year, and Mum will keep the council in check. We'll all lean on each other; I have everything covered."

"Frederick? You spoke to the council, then, about me returning?" she asked, chewing her lower lip in contemplation.

"Once I told them I wouldn't take the position without you, they were most understanding. Mum also convinced them. Your speech in the townhall might have helped soften their resolve."

She was grateful for their forgiveness. It all made sense on paper, but in practice, she wasn't so sure.

"What about managing the list?" she asked, needing all the facts before she decided.

"My mother wouldn't have anyone touch the list but her," he said, and she could see how much he wanted it to work. "Lou is even recruiting outside help from the village to help decrease the workload. The responsibility doesn't have to all be on me."

"But if you weren't with me, you could stay in Yule indefinitely," she protested.

He wrapped his arms around her and held her close, not letting her escape.

"I'd rather lose everything than lose you. All I want is you. That's why I'm giving you this. The bell is yours to use – you can come and go as you please in a moment's touch. There won't be a night where you aren't in my arms," he said, taking her face in his hands. She so desperately wanted to believe him.

Before she lost herself in him, she took a step back. "Can I think about it? I need to think..." If he held her a moment longer, she would throw the company aside and stay with him forever – but she was responsible for the company as much as he was responsible for Yule.

"Alright," he said, though she heard the anxiety in his voice. "I'll wait for you by the clock tower in Yule at dawn. Ring the bell and think of me. If you come, I'll know your answer, and if you don't... then you won't have to see me again."

Lyla watched him leave, taking her heart with him. But she had to think properly about this. She wasn't only changing the course of her life, but his as well.

CHRISTMAS DAY

Sitting by the Christmas tree with a mug of tea, Lyla wondered what it would be like to be Mason's girlfriend – wife. The split lives, the secrets; how she would never be able to tell her friends, her father, the truth. *What if I agree and then it doesn't work? What if losing him now is better than losing him later?*

"I can't," she said to herself, wiping her eyes, trying not to smudge her mascara. She had already lost her mother; her father was a distant thought. She was comfortable alone. Having a long-distance relationship full of secrets was the last thing she wanted.

She left the bell on the tree and went upstairs. She needed to say goodbye for both their sakes.

Jones jumped up on the bed, and a jingle filled the air as he coiled onto her lap.

"What have you got?" Lyla asked, and then she saw the silver bell hanging from his mouth by its red ribbon. She looked at the clock: 8:45pm. It would be 11:45am in Yule.

"You think I should go to him?" she said, and Jones stared at her. "I want to go! I don't want to be without him, but – it's complicated."

8:50pm. She took the bell from Jones and went back downstairs to hang it back on the tree. When she opened the door to the sitting room, the clock rang. The heavy dongs of the old grandfather clock in the hall filled the house, as if mocking her decision. She paused, and Jones weaved through the half-open door.

"I knew you would hesitate," Mason said, appearing before the Christmas tree.

He hadn't even waited a minute. She hated that he knew her so well. He was wearing the cable-knit sweater with a Santa Claus on the front. The irony made her smile.

Watching him from the doorframe, she realised that all she'd done was create two broken hearts. Without thinking, she ran to him, and he embraced her tightly.

"I'm sorry. I couldn't go to you. I was so afraid of losing you that it was easier to let you go," she said into his shoulder, only to hear him laugh.

"You know, that makes no sense. Plus, I've decided that I'm not going to overthink this," Mason said, putting her down, wiping the smudges of mascara from underneath her eyes.

"What if we fight? We always fight!"

He answered her with a kiss, and that was all the comfort she needed.

"I'll happily spend the rest of my life fighting with you. There's no losing me. We'll make this work. I promise you," he said in between kisses, and she wrapped her arms around his neck.

"I want to be with you. Today, tomorrow – even if I have to wait until Christmas every year, it will always be you," she told him. Resting against his chest, she could hear his racing heart as they held each other

"I'll never let you go again," he whispered.

And in all the years that followed, he never did.

OTHER COMPLETED WORKS

Young Adult Dark Fantasy | A Hellish Fairytale Trilogy

Crowned A Traitor

Where Traitors Fall

When Traitors Rise

Discover more from Kate Callaghan...

Get a FREE copy of Crowned A Traitor when you sign up for Kate Callaghan's Mailing List.

https://BookHip.com/PQZBACC

CROWNED A TRAITOR

Heir to Hell and the Dark Forest of Malum, Klara has been called upon to take her place as High Queen of Malum. Though Klara has no intention of ruling, her guardians want her head on a spike. Klara's only option - escape to Kalos, Fae ruled lands free from Dark Magic. To survive the perilous journey, she needs help...

A Leprechaun with a talent for smuggling.
A mischievous Demon with swaying loyalties.
The soul of a greying Warlock.
Lycaon siblings with a talent for deception.

Destiny has an awful habit of catching up with those who run.

ACKNOWLEDGEMENTS

TO YOU! Thank you so much for reading. I really can't do what I love without your continued support, and I'm grateful to every single one of you!

To Emma, for her magical editing skills. This book would be **nothing** without her.

Thank you so much to my ARC readers and Reader Group for hyping my stories.

Thank you to Cat for creating such a fabulous cover.

Thank you to Enchanted Ink Publishing for their wonderful formatting as always.

A special thank you to Ana-Maria and Kristen, for being my biggest supporters when it comes to me writing romance. I wouldn't have had the confidence to branch out without them hyping me up!

KATE CALLAGHAN

is an Irish fantasy author. Her debut young adult trilogy, *A Hellish Fairytale,* began with *Crowned A Traitor* in 2020. She is currently branching out into adult dark fantasy romance. She loves dark tales, villains, and happily-ever-afters – something you will find in all her books. Chatting with readers is her favourite part of being an indie author.

Follow below if you want to learn more about future stories! Signed copies are also available on the author's website.

Facebook Reader Group
Become A Rambunctious Raccoon

Mailing List | Gain Access To Exclusive News

WWW.CALLAGHANWRITER.COM

Instagram | @callaghanwriter

Tiktok | @katecallaghanwriter

Printed in the USA
CPSIA information can be obtained
at www.ICGtesting.com
LVHW031915101124
796239LV00010B/121

9781739753740